A R I A

GYORGY HENYEI NETO

ISBN: 9798730877443

This is for my family, who believes in me.

CONTENTS

Published by

Jostedalsbreen Publishing

Copyright © 2021 Gyorgy Henyei Neto

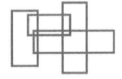

The characters and events portrayed in this book are fictitious. Any similarity to real persons, living or dead, is coincidental and not intended by the author.

PROLOGUE

Everyone's *pads* lighted up in the town, and a notification note read "ARIA foundation Announcement – Livestream".

Good morning all. My name is Doctor Anansi, and I am the lead designer and project leader at the ARIA foundation. It has now been six months since we started recovering from the terrible accident, we all came to know as the scintillance.

We at the ARIA foundation have been part of the town's community since its beginning. Building and investing in the city, energising the academic and creative centres, creating jobs and opportunities for you all, and keeping the region safe and flourishing. We have developed the most innovative and cutting-edge network of communication and entertainment in the state. We made sure that you were the first to experience all the convenience of pads, one of ours most celebrated products. We are glad to be part of such a powerful and resilient story.

As part of our mission, we have focused our energy into the reconstruction of the riverbank and all the areas affected by the accident. As of this moment, we have concluded the rebuilt and renovation of the train station, the market centre, and founded the ARIA's Engineering and Science Centre where the University once stood. Our next steps are to strengthen and remodel the old church and the watch tower, the historical elements that kept standing still, after the worst of times, after the scintillance.

The ARIA foundation is also glad to communicate that this year, even considering all the sacrifices and struggle all of us have been through, we have received a record number of students and professionals enrolled in our academic programs. As a thank you to your constant support, and as a token of our gratitude, we are happy to announce that all the over five hundred students are, as of this moment, recipients of the REBUILD fellowship, which will fund all the ongoing research projects for a period of five years, starting today.

And lastly, but by no means least, the ARIA foundation has chosen this great town to be the general headquarters of the newly remodelled space program, the Space Exploration and Expansion of Knowledge, or as it is more easily remembered, SEEK. The program development, as well as the funding, begins now, at the conclusion of this livestream.

Thank you for your attention, and from all members of the ARIA foundation, we hope to be always with you.

***

ON WAKING UP

I do remember the taste of the river coming out of my mouth, being pushed out, cursed, from the air trying to fit in my lungs. It was so much water, warm and acid, and scary. The light washed the darkness and engulfed my eyes. I gasped and smelled the damp air and the scent of moist dirt and grass. I felt so tired, all my muscles were worn, as dried tree branches, ready to break and fall. And I did fall.

The bright sky was partly hidden by the treetops, dancing slowly to the rhythm of the wind. My pupils followed the bounce of the leaves, and all started to spiral. The darkness flooded again, and the only light was the sliver of blue, gleaming from my own body.

***

Waking up in a bed felt alien. I opened my eyes and could not find the sky, the trees, the wind. There was only the ceiling and the silence. It took me a few breaths to realise what was happening. I was in someone's house, in someone's room, sleeping in someone's bed, dressed in someone's clothes. At least I was dry, and breathing was not an effort anymore.

I sat on the bed, not forcing myself to stand up, feeling my legs still shaking and my back sore. My chest. It was supposed to be ripped open...or was it? Had I just dreamed it? I didn't remember. I was with...Chris. Yes, I remember him. Chris, of course. It was his house, his bed, still someone else's clothes. But that didn't matter, I knew where I was, and I knew he would be there with me.

My head was hurting too, a weird, foreign pain. I was not used to drown in the river, so it was only logical that the pains and aches I was feeling were not the common ones. That didn't matter either. I needed to go and talk to him, to know what happened.

But I didn't go. I didn't have to. Because from the other side of the slightly open door, I heard steps, coming and going, never coming too close, and never too far. He's here, I thought. Should I say something? Should I prepare? I stood, in the middle of a dimly lit bedroom. I searched for the loo. Suddenly I realised I was again full of water.

The bathroom had a scent of pine and chemicals, recently cleaned. The sink and the mirror were hugely ornate. I looked at myself, framed in gold and iron. I was pale, sunken cheeks, dark, deep eyes, and the long, scruffy, wild hair that has avoided a brush for far too long. I never brushed, not my thick, brown locks, impossible to contain. No, it was to be let free, so I did. I touched my chest, by impulse, a memory, and didn't find a thing.

"It was a dream then", I said to myself only, "the light, the scar...Chris too?"

I could not remember what happened, not entirely. The last day, the past few days were less than a blur, barely a puff of smoke, impossible to hold. But there was something still there, before that. Yes, this was not Chris's, it was someone I knew. Names don't come to me easy, but she lives here.

The sound of the door opening made me lose my train of thought. It opened, and the faint light from the other room flooded slowly into the darker bedroom. Under the door frame, only a silhouette was visible. Not of Chris, but of a woman. I thought I recognised her.

"Dia, you woke up", she said, surprised and glad, a voice I knew.

***

Carrie and I sat at the dining table, facing each other. After I finished eating as much as I could, we stood there, in silence, for a long time, or maybe a few seconds. What should I have asked? Who are you? Where am I? Can I have more food? All those questions seemed reasonable and necessary, but I decided to ask the most obvious question.

"What happened?"

"You slept for four days. Do you remember anything?", she asked back, almost as if she hadn't heard my question.

"No. I don't think so. Images maybe", I said. "Do you know what happened?", I probed.

"We found you by the river, passed out. We brought you back home", she continued. "We were looking for you after you didn't come back home. It was dark and late, and we thought you were... gone", did she mean dead? "We hoped you would be coming back in the morning", maybe not dead then.

"We only decided to go out and look when your pad did not respond. We were worried", Carrie said.

When was the last time I saw Carrie? She took me in, after mum died. She used to say they were sisters from another time, whatever that meant. Regardless, she was there since I could remember, remember now or earlier, a memory of a memory. She was there when mum was no more. After that, memories are shattered, sparse, and in disarray. I saw her yesterday, or that one day's yesterday, and it feels as if I died and returned, another person, looking for old Dia's memories and past.

"We?", I asked, still feeling the light bothering my eyes.

"Yeah, Mal came with me. I needed her. I didn't know if I could bring you back myself", Carrie lips parted, and she dropped a sigh.

"Mal", I repeated, tasting the name, tossing around my mouth. It felt familiar. "Is she…?"

"No, she went back home now", Carrie pulled the air, and it almost looked as if her eyes were moist.

Even in her nightgown, with no makeup, short, silver hair pulled up held by half-set pins, she was beautiful. The memories returned as a breeze. Her thin lips smiled a grateful and yet mysterious smile, and her eyes, great blue marbles in large round frames, starred at me as if I were a strange, an animal, something uncanny and that should not have been. Her gaze questioned me.

"Do you remember anything Dia? Of what happened to you?", Carrie finally asked again.

I shook my head. Maybe that was actually a dream. Chris. I haven't seen him in years.

Carrie smiled again and slid something over the table towards me. A tin box, no label, no writings, just a plain box. She nodded at me, and said, "take one, it will help with your head"

My head? I didn't have a headache anymore, and the sickness left me as soon as I ate. "It's fine Carrie, I don't need, I'm okay now"

She pushed the box closer, "It can help with the dreams"

***

A few weeks passed since I had woken up. My head was being flooded with sights and images of my past, names, places, events, conversations, mum.

I spent most of the days at home, recovering. Carrie said it would be for the best, since I suffered a violent trauma, and perhaps going back out too early could get in the way of my memories return. At first, I did not mind. Her apartment was huge. I had my own room, my stuff was brought from the University's dorm, and even though I was feeling better, a weakness still lingered, grabbing me by the feet from time to time, and dragging me.

We would spend most evenings talking about me, about my work at uni, about my friends. I still could not place names and faces in the same person, and when they came to my dreams, they would never talk. The only other person I remotely remembered was Mal.

Mal would come by a couple of times a week. Being a nurse, she wanted to keep an eye on me, check if I was getting better. She was always interesting to be along with. As far as I could place myself in my own memories, I was a terribly private and introvert person. I liked to talk to Carrie, and every day, more and more, the memories of me and mum chatting would come back. But besides them, I felt that it was hard to be open. People did not need to know everything that went through my head. But Mal was the closest to my polar opposite. While I was skinny and tall, she was short and, well, not skinny. She was loud, extravagant, joyful, caring, tea drinker.

She was closer in age to me than Carrie's, but the two of them definitely had much more in common with each other than any of them with myself.

"How are you hon? Are you feeling better? Is she feeding you enough? Oh hon, you're still looking so thin. Look at those cheeks. Let me see the eyes, open up", she grabbed my head, and pulled the skin under my eyes, opening them to the light and the air, stinging and drying them. "Hm, you look fine. But you have to keep resting and building up energy alright? Oh my, look at the time", she sipped her tea, and chomped on a piece of the lemon cake. With her mouth full she announced, "I have to go, hon. My class is starting…oh dear, I don't even want to see. I'll pass by some other time, okay? Ta", she said, kissing my cheeks. She turned to Carrie and did the same, "Mrs Carrie, keep an eye on her, and if you need anything let me know"

Carrie nodded and smiled briefly. Almost at the door, Mal turned and said, "Dia, completely forgot. Oh, this head of mine, getting old", she chuckled. She was barely a couple years older than I was, and she was feeling old. Was I wrong nothing feeling old? Mal continued. "Adonis asked about you. Do you...remember him already?"

As I heard the name, a dam broke, and it flooded my brain some more. "Adonis", I said. The name was easy to say, as if I had created muscle memory for it, as if I had spoken it. "Yeah, maybe. I think", another name came to my mouth, a bit bitter and less known, less used than the first, "He has a sister...V...Vóra?", yes, that was it. I smiled broadly, without noticing.

Mal giggled again, "Oh Dia, yes, Adonis and Vóra. Oh, they'll be happy to hear from you. Well, Adonis will for sure", the last part she almost whispered, so only herself could hear. "Anyway, I have to go". She shut the door behind her.

Carrie turned to me, looking both surprised and curious "Interesting. You remember them?"

"I do", I said simply.

"Did you dream about them?", Carrie said it raspier, quieter.

"No, not yet I think", I replied, uncertain. Maybe I had.

"We can verify", she grabbed the tin can from the breast pocket of her jacket, and from it, produced a white, circular pastille, a capsule. She called it *mints*. "Do you want to try again?"

With palm turned upwards, I drew my hand, and she filled it with one of those *mints.*

***

ON DREAMS OF
MEMORY

The dream was familiar. It came at night, in the darkest of the hours, like an insomniac lover, and it touched me, it played with me, it held me in its many arms, many fingers, many eyes watching me sleep, and the many mouths speaking in many tongues, and many ears hearing me softly breath, softly whimper, and the many noses smelling my neck and my chest, and the back of my spine, and it moves up, up towards my neck, and my head, and my hair.

When I woke up, the dreams still did not make sense. Only images, one image, of light, a pillar of blue light, straight up towards the sky. I looked and looked at it, and if I closed my eyes, palinopsia would stain it into my mind, even in the dark.

Weeks went by, after I began to remember, and the dreams were becoming less iconographic and more subjective. Those were my dreams of memory. I had them often. My mother would show up on them, and our house, and we would be sitting in our bench, and she would be holding something up, towards the sun, and the light would then take over. A blue light, just like the pillar.

With help and patience, I managed to get to know that place, to get friendly with my counteractors, and to position myself actively in the scene. There was my old house, my mom's workshop, dusty, full of rust and metal, the large green anvil right next to her tall wooden desk. The desk, used, battered, battled, and lived in, holding chisels, hammers, pliers in its niches. A small, flickering light stood valiant at the edge of the desk, trying to offer some brightness to the now darkening space. "The artificial light lies" mom would say, when she was checking her work, "only the sunlight can show your work and your mistakes". When she wasn't inside working on her pieces, she would sit outside with a cup of dark and steamy coffee and would contemplate her mistakes. "See here?", pointing to her latest incision on a bracelet or brooch, invisible to the untrained eye "that's where I slipped. Here, you see? There was a bump in the metal vein". She saw impossible things, and she did impossible things. "No one can see that mom, don't worry", I would say, trying to be helpful and supportive, but at the same time implying that I also could not see the scratch. "That's not the point Dia", she corrected me, "the point is to watch your hands, watch your material, watch your tools, and learn. You have to learn the language of the materials".

I still couldn't hear her voice in the dream, no words, however. At this point things had shape, and I could get close to them, but the sounds were muffled.

The last time I dreamed this dream, I saw the *pads*, all the *pads* in the house, shouting, screaming for attention, beeping and blinking, another layer of noise that I could try separate and investigate. Images were clearer. I saw a news anchor, panic in the streets, another was showing mobs and protests, the next one showed the ARIA foundation's building, as it stood then.

I tried to talk, to reach her, to touch her. But no matter how I tried to force myself to move, whichever reach I managed with my arms, she was far. Constantly far, always far enough, and close enough. She muttered something and was showing something in her hands. We were outside, seating on our wooden bench, side by side. I could see her signature on the side of the bench, her style, her gracious and strong movements, the precise and organic design. I could smell the coffee. She held the object high against the now clouded sky. The mutter was about natural light and mistakes and revealing. She was happy, fulfilled, complete somehow, seating there with me. And the light.

***

Dreams of memory. Whose memory were those?

She told they were mine, and I believed her. There was no reason not to. But I didn't feel like they were mine. I could see myself in them, my mother, and yet, I couldn't remember the feeling of living it. I suppose one does not remember being a baby. I tended to brush this feeling off. It was normal, she said, and others did too. Some sort of selective memory loss, to suppress traumatizing events. I had to believe that people would be affected by the accident that blew up half of the town and dug a crater in the middle of the river. That could be considered traumatic, in the least.

Even then, I felt as if I was being robbed of those memories somehow. By happenstance or design, parts of me were lost, or taken away.

And Carrie was helping me bring all that back to the surface, back to focus. She was the first person I saw after the *scintillance*'s fog disappeared from my eyes and my mind. She was there, the first memory from after I woke up. Carrie brought me home, took care of me, helped me put the pieces into place, at least the pieces I had, which weren't many. When I came in, she said, I only knew my name and was babbling about a blue light. The *scintillance*, people say, had a blue gleam. So, we put another piece together, and concluded that I saw the *scintillance* and that was what could have put me in that state.

For days I slept, and during that sleep I began to

see things, things that looked and felt like memories. They were violent arrays of images, lights, sounds, and different types of pains. When I woke up, my heart was racing, my brain was bursting out of my head, and my whole body was aching. Carrie gave me one of her mints and told me that she found me by the river, wet and cold, by myself, which probably led to a pneumonia. Not a strong one, and I was recovering. She asked my name, and I said "Dia", which confirmed her suspicions from my original mumbling. She then asked me if I remembered anything else, and I didn't, not even the light. My mind was blank. It was becoming less blank.

***

I started going out of the house more, jogging by the river, after they finished rebuilding the pathway. It followed the riverside, rushing rapid from the west. The river was always lush and green and misty in the morning, and hot in the afternoon. It would then snake and twist in rhythm with the riverbank, tossing and turning, climbing down the long downhill, until it reached the foundation campus. One could see the offices and classrooms facing the river. I felt the jealously sights on me while I ran, fast and sweaty, while others were trying to survive whatever lecture or workload they were suffering. The path continued, and when it reached the crater, it would edge it, circling around it, to again meet the river on the other side. Running was a free mind activity. I would leave my brain in autopilot and enjoy the burning sensation flowing through my legs with every step, the vibrations of the muscles and bones, the breathing flow in symmetry with my pace. I enjoyed the view, but during those moments, it was background noise, like a paint in a restaurant. It eased my eyes, my ears, and my heart would be the slave of my legs and my feet. Background noise, while my brain worked on something by itself, which I would then digest and rethink afterwards.

A single line of thought however decided to follow my route and run along with me. I was thinking of coincidences, of serendipity, of happenstance, of fate even. All that started to juggle and bubble inside, creating shadows in front of my eyes. "Stop" I said. Shook my head, stretched and hit the side of my thigs. And there I went again. By the river, by the footpath, by the crater and my memory of what it was.

The rain started and began to soak the ground all around the crater. On sunny, warm days like that, the rain always came at the edge of light, when the warmth drove all the steam and vapours from the atmosphere, collected and parcelled in the sky, and scattered the water back at Earth, in a cycle, almost ritual reverence from the sky to the ground, and from the ground to the sky, and the cycle continued, as the flow, as the water, as the rain. And it fell.

It was warm. Full and bloated drops of water in deep dive from the clouds that circulated the foundation building. A grey carpet, undulating from dark patches of wet mould to silver slivers of light, to pink and orange hues. But there was no rain that could suffer the parched crater. It was dry, rotten, undead, and perfectly still, in time and space. Not even the rain, nor he clouds were allowed in that circle of desolation.

And I stayed there for how long it was the time that it was supposed to be. I watched the rain clean the town, fill the river, and soak my hair. I saw the clouds moving, slowly and heavy, jettisoning the water it gathered, and still, avoiding the area surrounding the impact. I was used to that sight. How many times I sat in the same place, just watching, catching my breath from running? It was trivial now, and it was not surprise I felt. It was consent. I agreed with those clouds, as they missed the perimeter of the crater, as if the *scintillance* created an invisible pillar, a stake stabbed into the chest of the planet.

I thought about my mother. I walked to the river. Wet my feet, my whole leg. The river changed they, so much different now. It was wilder, curvier. The crater shifted its trajectory, but in exchange, gave it more movement. It twisted and turned, through the hole. Nothing grew in that place. I felt the water go through my legs, through my chest, I walked in unstable mud and rock. I could still see the woods that backed our house. They were all there, they have always been there. A silence army of bent pine. But no house, no workshop, no wooden bench. The small garden in the back, half charred and dead, a crocked tree. Were those things actually there?

Loss for something I don't remember, is a little like hunger, it only stops when the presence is eaten, but sometimes the feeling is so deep, that mere presence is not enough. The memory wants to absorb me whole, an eagerness to be within the past, within the other, in a single unification. The most urgent feeling that life can provide. I miss things I am not sure I have ever lived, things that I don't know if they have ever been mine. I need to feel that that belongs to me. The house, the memories, the dreams, all that. All of that. The river flows, it goes through the crater now.

***

I came back late. The dreams seemed to have taken their time to be digested, so I thought it would be good to burn them as much as I could.

"Dia, is that you?" Carrie asked from the kitchen, as I failed to open the door silently. "There's some food left still. I was waiting for you, but I was hungry, and I had a meeting *overpad*, so I had to eat by myself before it."

Carrie was helping me get back to my feet. For six

months now, since I woke up, she has been caring for me, slowly going through my dreams and my memories, trying to piece together who I was and how did I end up drowning in the river. My name was the only thing I had in me when she found me, but now I could clearly see some of my past before the *scintillance*.

"Thanks Carrie, yeah, I'll have something" I didn't realise how hungry I was. "Sorry, I was jogging. I thought it would be nice to go for a run by the river again" I tried to bring that as direct and smoothly as possible. I knew that she was still worried about me going to the river, but I couldn't avoid it forever, so I was pushing myself to go to places in my memory and try to understand them.

She popped her head through the kitchen door, as I was biting some of the bread and pouring the still warm coffee. "The river?" She asked, curious and upset. "What did you find there?"

"Nothing. Just the river, and the crater, and things being built, just that" I haven't talked about the house, my mother. "It was just a run Carrie, it's fine. I'm fine"

Carrie then came out to the living room, she still had her hair up and was wearing a button-up shirt, maybe because of the meeting, and her old, dotted sleeping trousers, because the meeting was overpad. "Look, you know you can do whatever you want, and I know I get annoyed when you go out to the river, but you do understand that is just because I worry, right?" Her voice was flat, as it normally was, but her tone was off. I knew all that, and I knew I got her upset.

"I know" I spoke in between bites. "And I'm sorry, I should've said. But I am feeling so much better. Been days that I have genuinely been having more energy, more than I can ever remember having in my whole life. I just want to go out and start again, you know?"

"I do" She sighed and smiled. "You didn't tell me about your dreams today. Do you want to do it now?"

"Yeah, that'll be great" I finished eating and we moved to the chairs next to the window.

***

The dream diaries, we called. I would talk about my dreams, what I had seen, what new visions, symbols, people I have met, and we would try and put those pieces together. Her mints helped. She told me they were developed by the foundation, part of their health department. They produced the majority of the products and consumables we used in town, and medicine wasn't the exception. People would complain that the foundation were holding a monopoly in the region, others would praise the company for their effort to distribute necessity products to everyone equally.

"They haven't finished testing on those mints yet?" I asked.

"No" She said, blowing a jet of smoke through the open window. "Not yet. Still only for internal consumption"

She handed me one, and I swallowed. And the dreams returned.

"Do you think I am ready to go back to the university?" I asked, already falling into that another dimension, the one I where I would stop feeling my body, the one where I could look down and see myself seating in the chair by the window. "I really want to go back. I miss it, you know. The department, research...mom" My eyes were heavy, and I let my head drop sideways.

"I can see my mum. We are in the workshop. I remember that. That is my real memory. She is much younger there, she looks like me, I think; I must be nine or ten then. But I look at myself, I'm at the age I'm telling this. She is saying something, inaudible, there is too much noise. She keeps hammering. I can only grab a few words – scar, knife, river – they don't make sense, but so much of what she is saying is being muted. I can't see her face, she is facing the window, in front of her desk. She is hammering something over the anvil. Her ancient, green anvil, given to her by some relative. With the thongs, she holds the metal being worked. Sparks come out, but they are blue. She turns and drowns the piece of glowing metal in the water. It hisses in pain and agony. It breaks and it twists, and everything is hammered back into place" I breathed "She is going outside, holding the piece of metal out in the sun. She's talking about...mistakes? The sunlight. Yes, I remember that too" And then all ended. I blinked and saw myself in the chair. I blinked again, and I saw Carrie in front of me, waiting.

"Hey, are you back? Is that all?" She hands me a glass of water.

"That's all. I could almost see her. It's getting so close; I can almost touch her" I lower my head in between my legs and gasped. "Shit, I'm still hungry Carrie".

She shrugged and just nods towards the kitchen. "There's plenty still".

I brought back some more of the dark, nutty bread she loved so much, and the salty cheese, and a bottle of wine, and two glasses. "Here" I handed her one of the glasses.

We ate and drank.

"Do you remember things from before Dia? Before the *scintillance*?" Carrie questioned.

"Yes, I think so. There is a lot of fuzziness still, events are blurred, and specifics are pretty much non-existing. I remember glimpses, a swift light between a multitude of rain clouds. I can see my mom, I can vaguely see Mal, and Adonis and his sister too, but nothing very particular about them. I do remember the university, and some of the people...their names run away from time to time, but I remember their faces. And I remember the house. More like a feeling than actually a memory of something happening" I paused for a moment, considering what I was going to ask "What happened at the house, do you know? I passed by where I know where it should have stood, but there are only a few walls standing, the area is flooded, and there's this crooked tree".

She should have expected that I would try and find things for myself as well. "You went quite far on your run" Carrie pointed. "Well, my guess is the *scintillance*. It brought the whole university and the ARIA office down completely. I'm surprised that there are still walls for you to find" She looked distressed.

I didn't probe anymore, but she decided to keep going.

"I don't want you to think that I am keeping you from carrying on with your life. My wish is for you to recover as fast as humanly possible, so you can go out and finish that degree and find a job, so you can help with rent" She chuckled. "For all I know, I would love for you to just go and find all there is to find about yourself. And I am trying to help" She sighed quickly. "You're an adult and I have no right to keep forcing you to wait for you to recover all your memories before you can carry on and restart. So, I have decided" I was again caught mid-chew "I will call the foundation and organise everything so you can restart your degree. Tomorrow"

I swallowed the bread and pushed it down with a sip of the wine, and simply said "Thank you Carrie" She raised her glass in agreement.

***

ON RESTARTS

The foundation was tremendous. I looked out of my window in the morning as I was leaving to begin again, and I could see its tall structures pointing up, like fingers pushing from the ground below shooting up to the skies. The glass and metal shapes stood out from the rest of the town, perhaps intentionally. The tallest building in town before the *scintillance*, and before the reconstruction, was the watch tower, one of the few that survived the incident. It was tall, but nothing compared to what has been built where the rest of the university once was. It covered the view we had, even from the top of the hill, of the river, the crater, and the pine forest further away. In comparison, the watch tower, and the old church attached to it, were irrelevant, a non-presence.

There is this feeling that comes from your stomach, that crawls up your throat, clenching and clutching, and it climbs up to the back of your mouth, and you know that if you gasp, if you so much as breath, that hand will close in a fist. I swallowed it and walked down the hill.

There were building sites and working being done in every second house and street. All the way down, everywhere I looked, there were scaffolding being put up, builders passing by with safety hats, and construction signs advising a detour due to workings undergoing ahead. The town was bustling, being rebirthed and remodelled. And in all of them, the ARIA logo. The foundation was everywhere. In reconstructing the area destroyed by the *scintillance*, in our *pads* and networks, and in our food and medicine. Some said they owned the town, that somehow, they have purchased the whole area, along with its infrastructure and population, and are using it as a testing ground for a new technology or material. Some believed something similar, but the reasons would be much more trivial and mundane, things like tax evasion and monopoly control. I didn't know what to believe yet. In all honesty, I didn't want to believe in anything, not yet, not before I could know more about myself first.

Carrie told me to meet with Mal and a couple of other people at ten in the morning. I stood at the green in front of the giant letters spelling ARIA, and pulled my head back, trying to look at the top of the building. People came and went, and I felt more like a lost child, rather than a graduate student. With a long and deep breath, I nodded to myself and walked through the blue tinted glass, leading to the foundation's main hall.

I was greeted by three people. Three faces I have met before, one of them I could even remember the name.

"Mal?" I said cautiously.

"Oh, hello Dia!" She came closer and held both of my hands. "How are you hon? Are you feeling okay? Oh, it's been so long, I was so worried, we all were. We talked to Ms Carrie, she told me you were coming, and I was so happy. Oh dear, it was so good to see you. You look so much better than..." She stopped, noticed she might have stepped too far. She was the only other person who saw me when Carrie first found me. Being a nurse made her the first and best option. "Oh, my dear, never mind" She pulled me towards the other two.

I have seen their faces. They appeared in my memory dreams from time to time, but I didn't know their names, and I didn't asked Carrie also. It was my choice, I didn't want to be handed the names of people I have known, I wanted to find them again myself. From the three of them, I could only remember Mal's.

"Hello" I waved shyly. "I'm sorry. I know I know you both, but I don't remember much. Adonis and..." I thought that made me good with faces but not with names. Maybe I wasn't good with people.

The woman appeared to be the same age as me and Mal, but she was shorter than me and leaner than Mal. And he, he looked plain, nothing particularly distinct, other than his glasses and his ruffled blonde hair. The only thing interesting, tremendously interesting in fact, were his eyes. Dark grey, almost silver in the right light, and a brush of quick blue floating around its irises. I felt myself drowning in that pool of darkness.

"Hi Dia...ahn, Adonis yes,...I'm Adonis. I mean... my name is...it's fine. Don't worry" He stumbled in his words, and maybe I was actually remembering, it felt so natural, as if I knew he would, as if I expected him to.

"So, what can you remember then? You remember Mal's name, and you remember our faces. What else? Do you remember what happened to you already? Maybe not, right? Convenient I guess" His sister. Yes, she was Adonis' sister. Aggressive and hard. I also felt that as quite usual for her.

"Vóra!" Mal rebated. "Don't say that. She is still recovering from a really nasty accident. You should be helping us here. If you don't want to be here, you don't have to" she didn't do a good job pretending to be angry.

"No, I do Mal. I do alright? We just don't have the whole day to waste with you" Vóra said that directed to me.

"Vóra" Her brother also intervened. Vóra then gave up, threw her hands up and walked off. I followed her with my eyes until she disappeared beyond one of the glass doors. I couldn't stop noticing her subtle limping.

"Is she okay? Did I do anything?" I had the feeling I had actually done something to her. But as her name, I couldn't see that in my memory.

"Oh hon, don't worry about Miss Temperamental over there. She is fine, she is just confused also, by having you back after so long, it is a change for all of us" I felt the heat burning my cheeks and ears. "Oh no! I meant a good change dear, a very good change. Right Adonis?" Mal looked at him, asking for assistance.

"Ahn...yes, yes of course...a nice change" He managed a half smile.

"Alright, let's go then. Come dear, this way" Mal grabbed my arm, and we walked side-by-side, heading to what it seemed one of the few hallways not under construction or going through repairs. "This building is still being finished. You know, some interior design here, some painting there. It's the newest part of the foundation, hon. They want to have it ready for when they start that space program of theirs. Oh, have you watched Doctor Anansi speaking? She is great. Maybe you get to meet her soon" I didn't have a second to have a word into what Mal was saying. I looked back and Adonis was following us. He lifted his eyebrows and gave me a solidarity smile. I smiled back. I wished I could remember more of them.

***

Some memories came as a dam breaking, flooding a vale, washing through all that was under it, overwhelming at points. Others, however, came as drops. Single, solitary drops from a ceiling full of rainwater, but never cracking. The drops did hit hard, precise, and loudly annoying too.

Adonis arrived first. Only at face in the beginning, a bodyless mask. Then, floating in the nothingness, tendrils of flesh and colour formed from the bottom of his head, making up limbs and clothes, and he was there in front of me. And his eyes, closed at first, then slowly opening, turning from dull grey metallic to an engulfing blue glow. He was afraid, scared of something happening in front of him. Standing where his eyes were aiming to, I turned to look behind me.

Mum was there, holding liquid light.

I swung my head back towards him, and we were not in the nothingness anymore. We were at a classroom, an office perhaps, colourful light shone from the lancet shaped windows. The vision was static, unmoving, only but me. I scanned the room, everything stuck on their last movement. Adonis was there, arms crossed, sat on one of the chairs, looking at someone else speaking. A woman, young, pretty, short dark hair, frozen in mid-swing. More people around us three. Mum was standing next to me, gesturing at what Vóra was saying maybe. And in the back, someone else stood, back turned to the argument going on in the room. Long, large, wild hair, wearing what looked like a white lab coat.

A twitching inside my head, shaking everything in my view but me. Everything vanished with the last jolt, and I was back in the dark. Adonis was also back, his eyes flickering blue light, but now he was accompanied by another figure, Vóra, his sister. She stood just above Adonis, kneeling with one leg, protecting her face with her arm. The image stopped in a frame showing sparks and pieces of teared and torn clothing, and in Vóra's leg a wound, a slice shining the same light as his brother's eyes.

The light behind me, the light my mum held began to falter, dying out slowly, steadily, even though nothing else moved, only me. Only felt the heaviness of something in my hand, a blade of blue light.

Did you see that my dear? Did you see that? They are all there. Yes, they are. You are so peaceful, so sleepy. You are dreaming now. Look, you are desperately trying to catch those memories, but they are so flimsy, so plumy, far away, stuck in the ceiling. But that doesn't matter now. Close your eyes and open them again. Where we are now?

***

Being swallowed by memories and dream, I snapped back to reality. We spent a couple of hours going from floor to floor, laboratory to engineering office, hallway to hallway. They seemed too similar, I could barely position myself in that complex anymore, and not having windows only added to my disorientation. We stopped at another of the thousands – maybe more – automated glass doors, at the end of the longest corridor we had been all day. Mal produced her *pad* and moved in front of the panel next to the entrance. It beeped, and the doors slid, as all the others did. But different from all the other thresholds we stepped through, the other side of the glass was so different, and so familiar.

"And here we are, the old church. One of the two buildings in the whole university that survived the *scintillance*" Mal announced with gusto and pride.

The old church, as it was commonly known, was a large, vacant, high-ceiling cathedral, built millennia ago. It wasn't been used for its original purpose for almost as long. The university transformed it into a lecture hall, keeping the original aesthetic and preserving the frescos and statues of deities and gods that adorned the walls, doors, and pillars. I had slices of memories of that place.

That was not what was there on the other side of the glass door. The frescos, the statues, the carvings, and inscriptions, they were all stripped down, cleaned and brushed away. Rows of scaffolding and ropes were the only elements that differed from the white – or cream perhaps – painted walls, pillars, ceiling. The wooden floor was still standing, but tools and slides of wood carpets in one of the corners pointed to a full rehaul of the space. Stained glass windows. Those were kept. The faint light of the afternoon lit up the panels, and on their turn, they spilled a spectacle of colour and wobbly light, bringing a little life to the pale, sickly walls.

"And here is where you will be working Dia" Mal pointed to the desks and grey divisions, packed in one half of the hall, as the other half was already populated by painting and construction material. "They are renovating it at the moment, but you can come here anytime to work or to study" She didn't sound convinced. "Let's keep going?" And she pushed us both back to where we came.

"What about the pool on the back? I remembered mom and I went there a few times. I mean, I think I remember" I stopped and looked at her. "Is there a pool, right? I'm not going crazy, am I?"

"Yeah, there was a pool. It's still there...mostly" Adonis said, also being shoved out of the old church by Mal.

I left both of them where we first met, and walked around the foundation's complex, back to the old church's entrance. I wanted to see it from the outside, see if I remembered something, if something sparked any memory. It did not. The more I looked at the building, the grey concrete, burnt in parts, cracked in others, the more I tried to picture what the university was and what it might have looked like. Less than memories, just as the dreams, those were feelings. Feelings that I had been there, that I had walked these paths, stood by these woods, and had the shadow of the watchtower looming over me, as they did before, as the late afternoon sun accosted it from behind. So small in comparison with the rest of the new buildings. And such contrast.

The sun came down swiftly, but the orange and dark blue hue still shed some light into the world. I walked back, towards the glass monolith that was the main building of the complex. The lights from the windows and the cranes alike made it look more alive, but it did still have a taste of weirdness, of uncanniness. Not just the buildings, but the whole town. A metallic taste, fluid like mercury, but blunt and cutting, poking but never breaking the skin, only hashing it. And the crater behind it and beyond did not ease this feeling. People came and went, and they normally did and done, and none of them stopped to marvel or to be haunted but this view. Very adjusted already, I thought. Was I the odd one out? Definitely I was.

I put that behind me and started climbing up the hill. Balcony hills the road was called. It drove a snakelike wriggled route from the top of the neighbourhood, and dropped in the delta, forking in the road, splitting the traffic just as it hit the greens, and then the foundation watched over it. Sided by the lights of bars and pubs, an eventual construction site, temporary traffic lights, I made my way to the peak, with conflict afoot.

***

I have wondered, not often but also not just once either, how did Carrie find me, by the river. And why did she bring me in? I have never wondered that out loud, not directly to her, but I tried to probe it out. I questioned the happenstance, the unbelievable luck I had that she happened to be there at the exact time I climbed out of the water. I asked many times about the weather on that day, many times in different situations, just to confirm that the story remained the same. I queried also about the way she found me. Was I conscient, hurt, dressed? How long did she think I was underwater; did she think it was an accident, did she see anyone else around? I rotated the questions, their position, their sequence, and I never managed to get her to miss anything or to show any sign of doubt.

I trusted her, in the same way I trusted myself, my own memories and thoughts. I knew that they were there, and that everything they showed was true, or the true they believed in, but there was always something missing, a piece that didn't quite fit in the space it was designated. I continued to trust her throughout the whole six months we were living under the same roof.

At first, I was grateful, glad just to be alive and breathing. And the days went pass, and I grew more active and curious of what actually happened, but she pointed out that because I was still not completely healed, especially my memories, I should avoid restarting life, at least for a while. I didn't even know what life was before. It was all fuzz and confusion, so I gave in and agreed. I would stay, work on recovering my memories, and help her with her own projects. She even asked Mal to come in from time to time to both check on me and to be another person to talk. And Mal was the perfect choice, if talking was the need.

They worked together at the Health and Medicine department at the foundation, and they were researching this new line of mints. The mints I was using with Carrie were not the common mints people would buy at the pharmacy for headaches or back pain. Hers were beta-test version of a project that, as Carrie said, she couldn't tell me much about, because it was a secret, and she couldn't let corporate secrets be exposed. To whom? The foundation sells and makes everything. In any case, her secret mints were helping me concentrate and making me understand my dreams better.

"So, how was it?" She asked me as soon as I came in.

"It was fine. Mal and Adonis took me around the complex" I dropped my backpack, took my glasses and rubbed my eyes, and snored loudly. "that place is big. Fucking thing is gigantic".

"Did you see the office?" Carrie shrugged my language and took a sip of her tea.

"You mean the old church? Yeah" I replied careless while grabbing an apple. "They ripped the whole decoration inside. Bunch of scaffolding still there. It's great. And so fucking far from the rest"

Carrie pushed air from her mouth in disgust. "Don't be like that".

"Like what?" I played confused "I said it was great. What more do you want?"

She lifted from where she was, with her eyes closed she nodded. "I don't want anything. I found you a place to work, as you wanted. I made sure you have your own space, as you also wanted. I just...you know what? Forget. I don't even want to know".

I shoved the cracker and cheese in my mouth, open my arms, and in between chewing I said "Carrie! Carrie, I'm sorry. The place is great, it is. Look, I love it. I will be there every day, and I will think about you every time I hear them fixing the wood carpet or painting the walls".

She turned and pierced her lips, as she did when she wasn't been so serious.

I breathed deep and let it go, with a smirk "Thank you. I appreciate it".

"Just…never mind" She walked away and turned the living room lights off.

I ran after her and held her arm. "Carrie, wait. Come on"

"What?" She asked, now visibly upset.

"Look, I'm sorry. I was being stupid and bitchy. Can we…?" I pointed to the dark living room. She went first, turned the lights back on and sat where she was before. "Okay"

She drank a sip of her tea and refilled her cup with more of the brew in the pot.

"Where you actually going to leave your tea there, still hot?" I asked.

She lifted her shoulders and turned her bottom lip

"Maybe" She sipped again, now looking straight at me. "So, did you remember anything? From inside the complex, the foundation itself, the university site?"

I cleared my throat and sat and found that I had also forgotten my cheese and crackers by the side table. "No. I thought I had but was more like a feeling. Like a sensation I had been there more than actually being there. I have visions of that place, of the same architecture that the old church – my beloved office – but I think they are just loose pieces of things I still hold from my childhood".

"I see" Carrie had her notepad and pencil. "Anything else?"

I looked away, beyond her, the walls, all the way to the other side of the river. "No, I don't think so" She noted it down. "Well, actually…maybe…I have the vivid memory of me and my mother going to the pool, the one behind the church. Mal said it was still there, or parts of it. I haven't been there myself, but I want to. Maybe I can see something that might help".

Carrie nodded without looking up.

I sighed and asked, "Did you know my mother?"

The note taking stopped. "Of course Dia. We were…"

"Yeah, I know, 'sisters of another time'. You keep

saying that. What that even means?", maybe I was too harsh. Carrie glanced at me, confused and worried, anger perhaps in the depths of her greyish-blue eyes, "I want to know if you really did know here? Her wishes, her dreams? You never talk about her as a person"

If I didn't know, I could mistake her by a statue. Not a single movement, barely a breath. When she blinked, magically her movements returned, and she leaned back on her chair, leaving pen and paper on the desk. "I know she loved creating thing. She was an artist, you know?"

"Yeah" I swallowed another piece of the salty cheese "In my mind, in the memories I have, she was really an artist. A blacksmith by training, a jeweller by trade, a genius with the anvil and hammer. Her jewellery would be sought out by the people of all around the region. Rings, bracelets, small toys with intricate mechanisms that created the illusion that they were moving by themselves, flimsy and delicate garnets, and broches. She made a name for herself and gave us both a comfortable life. But her passion were knives. Sharp things, deadly and fast, and always beautiful" I found myself daydreaming, smiling.

I looked up, and Carrie had her head supported by her hand in fist, and she was staring at me, also smiling.

"Sorry" I said cleaning my throat. "Anyway, I want to go to the pool one of those days. To see it"

"Sure" Carrie replied.

***

ON ENCOUNTERS

The mornings were always colder down by the water, even during summer. The river controlled the temperature, and the pathway that followed its route would normally have dew clinging from the leaves of the pines, and mist would rise from the water, creating a curtain immediately behind the foundation's complex of buildings.

Since I learned about the pool, I have been building up courage to pass by it, to even run pass it. A whole week went by, and I ran or walked everyday by the river, on the path, behind the complex, but couldn't make myself go further behind the old church. Not after knowing that the half-demolished carcass of a building was the pool I wanted so much to visit.

After almost an hour running, I couldn't anymore. I had to stop. Too tired, too many thoughts. I managed to avoid hitting at least two people coming in the opposite direction. "Sorry", I gasped almost without sound. I stopped and sat on the grass.

I could see the crater from where I was, almost too close. Under the light it looked almost alive. Maybe it was the reflection of the glass panels from the foundation's buildings, or the heat evaporating from the surface of the water, but I could see the air, actually see the invisible cone of light that stood still where the crater opened the earth. Like particles of glimmering air itself refracting the reflected light of the midday sun. Scintillating pillar of sparkly air.

"You can run quite a lot" Someone said from above me. I were not wearing my glasses, and the salt in the sweat got in my eyes while I looked up to see owner of the voice.

"Sorry, do I know you?" I apologised, wiping my face with my shirt's sleeve. I looked up again, and a man stood, looking down, hand in his pockets, and what it looked like a silhouette of a smile. "I don't think I…"

"I'm pretty sure you do, Dia. Come on up" He held a hand and helped me get up. "Do you still remember this?" As my eyes adjusted, he pointed to his face, a white and pink scar and a slight wrinkle in his face, from his jaw up to his left ear.

I frowned and tried. Tried to remember something, someone, anyone. I wasn't good with names, neither with faces, but voices, those can touch the back of my soul and trigger things that were dormant. His voice was doing that. The more he spoke, the more I would feel my throat scratch and my heart beat fast, my eyes were moving fast, looking inside and beyond him, looking at pieces lost and forgotten. It wasn't a memory of dreams. Those are different, they are more intense, iconographical. That was not. It was emotion, a feeling. What is this feeling? Friend, friendship. Only one word came out in a gasp.

"Chris" I said and asked and exclaimed at the same time. I jumped, both my hands covering my mouth, my heart pounding, and my eyes hurting and stinging. I grabbed him and wrapped my arms around his neck, making his back bend. He was so tall. I didn't let it go and squeezed even harder. My eyes stung so much, and then they cried. His own arms now surrounded my body, holding me tight. We stayed like that for a minute. And I said "I remember you"

"That's good" He replied "I remember you too Dia. And I think about you, always"

I finally let it go and he smiled, stretching and cracking his back and neck.

"You almost broke me" And Chris laugh "Don't know if coming back was a good idea after all"

I laughed at that too, cleaning my eyes and my nose. "Asshole" I said and pushed him gently. "When did you get back? You...you grew up"

"I did, didn't I? You too grew old" He smirked and continued. "I got here just a couple days ago actually. I came to visit dad – it's his birthday next week – and I was just walking around, and I saw you running, so I stopped"

I looked at him, trying to ruminate in that fact, that coincidence. My mouth as open as if I would say something, but I didn't, I just kept thinking of coincidences.

"I'm joking Dia. I went to the university and asked if you were back. I met your friend Mal, is that it? And she told me you had come back to work" He pointed at the bench and we sat. "I think she even remembered me. I think I went to uni a few times with dad before…" He cleared his throat. "Anyway, I was going to uni again, by the river path, and – and that part is true actually – I saw you running"

"Right. Well, that's good. And how long are you staying? Have you been to your dad's yet?" I asked.

"I don't know yet. I'm staying with grandpa, but I don't want to bother him too much, his flat is already too small for himself alone, and I…well, I grew up right?" He laughed again.

It was contagious, not just the laughter, but being able to remember, without having to sleep and dream, without the mints. The images of Chris, of both of us, rushed through my head and travelled quickly by my eyes, each of them full and real, that

I could even touch. The scar.

"It got better" I said. He looked, puzzled, and I pointed to the left side of my own face, meaning his. "It doesn't look so bad. It looks…interesting" I tried a quick laugh.

He shrugged but smiled too. "Yeah. I think it actually suits my face if you ask me" He scratched the scar and blinked at me with one eye. "I think it makes me look even more handsome"

I laughed, loudly now, and he joined.

"Do you remember that day?" He asked, still laughing.

Yes, I did remember. I was jubilant that I did. It was clear as day. Memory is as bite. A jaw that jolts and takes a piece of yourself. It is a bite in the neck of history; it leaves marks, actions, perceptions, things that are not supposed to live in the past. Longing. A word is not enough to explain the feeling of loss, how to explain the expectation of a bite that never comes. It is not enough to explain the ache of loss, and the joy of finding.

"You left the house screaming and crying. Your face was smoking, and your fingers were trying to hold the blood and the skin on your face. People looked and chattered amongst themselves. Dogs barked, cats scrammed, all the world was watching the tragedy of Chris – the marked, the boy with the knife face, shard, blade, and the other names that the kids used. You ran so fast, so far, and so intently that day. We haven't seen you until later that night. Your dad had to come with you to ours, while my mom was trying to make me stop crying and letting me know that the whole thing was an accident, and that I would have to learn that eventually" He nodded, and I continued.

"You and your dad knocked, and we heard you both talking to one of the neighbours. I think your dad said something like "no Mrs Sinop, he's fine, it's just a skin wound, you don't need to worry. Just go back inside, is getting cold now" "

"Then mom opened the door, and you were there, so small, so fragile then. Your left cheek was protected by a large bandage, and your eyes were red and bulgy from crying too; and your lips trembling, shaking, as if the wind outside was moving them from side to side" I sighed, remembering. It was hard and sweet. "Mom crouched down, looked right at you and said, "does it hurt?", and you just closed your eyes and nodded up and down, and up again, vividly and firmly" I swallowed, cleaned my throat quickly, and moved on. "" Yes, I'm sure it does. I'm sorry okay? Those things are dangerous, and you children still don't know how to use those tools. She didn't do it on purpose, you know that right?", that's what mom said so amorously, so sugary. And you nodded again, less aggressively then. And then, to make you feel better, she said "tell you what. I will teach Dia how to use my tools, and I want you to come and learn too, what do you say?"

"I do remember that" He was looking at nothing, at the river. "I was so happy; I think I completely forgot about the pain. I just remember turning to dad and asking if I could"

"Did I even say sorry?" I tried to recall that.

"You did. I'm pretty sure you did. I said it was fine, or something like that" He helped me remember. "We never actually started that did we?"

"Maybe once, twice? You left shortly after" I wasn't smiling anymore. "How's your mum?"

He left his head bob back and forward again and sighed the longest and deepest sigh. "She's fine. Sad, still recovering, but fine" He stopped for a moment. "She's back to work too. So, that's an improvement"

"Yeah" I confirmed. "Have you been to your dad's already?" I asked one more time.

"No, not yet" He turned and looked at me "Do you want to come along?"

"Sure" I smiled sadly.

***

I left him do what he needed to do. I didn't want to

disturb, but also didn't know how to behave. The cemetery was one of the few spots that the scintillance had very little impact, just a few graves had been stirred, cracks in the main gate, and the light posts had to be swapped. Other than that, it looked as it always did, sombre and awkward.

"I thought this whole place would be inside the crater" Chris said, still looking at his father's headstone.

I didn't reply, maybe because I didn't know how to reply. I felt uneasy and ashamed. Chris came to town just to visit his father, and I couldn't even be bothered to know where my own mother was. Carrie wanted to take me, but I always refused. I was absolutely scared. Scared that if I saw her own tombstone, I will make it real, and I didn't want to make it real. For some reason, I believed that my mother was still out there, and that she was looking for me. Stupid dreams.

"I'm sorry Dia. About your mother" He finally turned to face me. "I should've come when it happened"

"That's fine" I murmured. "We didn't do anything. It's fine"

He stood in front of me, silent. "I need to tell you something. I didn't come just to see my dad. I came because of you. You are in danger Dia"

My jaw dropped of surprise, of absolute unexpectedness. What danger could I be?

"What?" I asked, waiting for him to tell me something different.

"Dia, you don't know, but you are being watched. The foundation, it is not what it looks like. Do you know what happened to my dad? To your mother?"

I stared at him, reactionless. "They…" I did not actually know the details. I knew that they were gone.

"The foundation. That happened, they killed them" He whispered.

"What!?" And I shouted. "What the fuck are you talking about Chris? Killed them? Are you losing it?"

"Look Dia, I know about you. That you don't remember anything that happened after the scintillance, and that your memory got messed up because of it. But you have to believe me, you have to. I came here to save you. We have to find where the knife is" Chris' behaviour changed completely. I didn't remember how he was, not entirely, but I knew that he was not like this. My mother killed? Finding a knife?

"Chris, stop it! What are you saying?" I couldn't remember him anymore.

"I'm saying that you have been lied and misled. When dad died, they told me that it was an accident. A peril of the trade, that's what they wrote in his file. I was never told what exactly happened that day. I asked, and mom also didn't know, but she was far, so our struggle didn't matter to them. "He stopped, dramatically "They were researching a new...thing, an element, a metal he said many times. Him and your mother. She wasn't a blacksmith, she was a physicist, they both were. This Gravitonium thing, dad said, was radioactive, very dangerous, but it could change our lives, everyone's lives. But I couldn't let him die with no explanation. I dug and I dug, and even though I knew I was putting myself at risk, I couldn't stop. And then your mom...I kept digging. And I found. I had all of dad's journals at home. He was paranoid about his work and his ideas, so everything was doubled. Until the very end" And again, another pause, for a deep sigh "In his notes, he said that the metal finally won, and as a gift, it would kill him slowly, painfully, but he couldn't stop, and he didn't. Until he lost"

"Chris" both my hands again covered my mouth. "I'm sorry, I didn't know"

"That's the point Dia" He snapped out of his emotional account. "No one did. Just the foundation, myself...and your friend Carrie"

My hands dropped, my muscles turned to jelly, and

my whole mouth dried out. "Do you know Carrie?"

"Yes, I do" He looked around, as if we were being followed, being watched. "Let me tell you what I know"

***

ON DOUBTS

When a heart skips a beat, time doesn't stop, time doesn't slow down or anything like that. When a heart skips a beat, it stings, it hurts, it's a punch in the chest, it pulverizes the moment of one's life. It's a dead moment. And after what Chris told me, my heart was stinging, and it hurt.

The sun was setting, making blue turn to orange, and then became black. There were so many stars in the sky. We walked by the river until the pathway was blocked by the edge of the crater. Chris wanted to see it, the building, the foundation's main complex. He had never seen it up close, not finished at least. "It's big. Bigger than in the photos". That was his only comment.

We walked back, up the hill, and through the narrow streets. It all seemed so different now. Maybe not different, but weightless. The building sites, the dirty road, the light posts revealing the cobble under our feet, all that was meaningless, compared to what we were involved. We got halfway up the road, and I asked, "do you have where to stay here?", in the hope that he also didn't have anywhere to go. But of course, he was staying with his grandfather. Forgot about it. I felt him making a move to ask me if I wanted to stay with them tonight, but I dismissed before he could say. "I can't", I said, "I need to ask her. I need to face this now; I don't want to wait anymore" to which he agreed, smiled, and walked off.

There was just so much in my mind now. My mother, Gravitonium, a knife, radioactive, death. Why were they trying to hide that? What else were they hiding? And Carrie too? How could she not tell me any of that, after all that time? And the mints. She was drugging me, making sure I would remember something related to my mother, and the metal. Fuck.

And she told them. About me, my memories, my dreams. Why didn't Chris tell me earlier? He could've come earlier, couldn't he? Fuck, fuck.

***

In the living room, she vomited those words back to me, like she was holding something strange inside her, and her body was now rejecting it. I felt disgusted. She knew and didn't told me. That vomit on me. I tried to clean myself.

I fell in the chair. Carrie was looking at me, hands hiding her wavy, trembling lips, trying to find me, to find my gaze. I didn't meet hers. She never cried. Not for serious things. Whilst reading a book, watching a play, but not really. Not for life and the shit that happened in it.

It took what it felt like millennia to ask.

"Did you tell them? Did you actually tell them? About me, my memories? About mum?" I made my voice lower, tenser.

"Yes" she said simply.

"My memories Carrie! Mine!" I was hating myself for opening with her, for trusting her all that time. It took me so much to not be scared of talking about that. I told her the hidden meanings of our house, talked about my mom's workshop, about our bond, our life. I wished I said that. "I shared them with you because I needed help, because I was afraid and alone and had barely any idea of who I was. I came to you by chance. Something brought me here, to a safe space. I thought it was a safe space" My voice was a crackle, no more than noise.

"Dia, it is. It is still safe. I helped you heal, I helped you bring back those precious memories of the past, of your mother, of her work, your past. We were making progress"

"It wasn't your right. They are mine" I shouted.

"Our memories. I was there when you first remembered, or have you forgotten?" There it was, the Carrie I knew, argumentative, aggressive even.

Serendipity. There are words that appear in the moment they are needed. They are not ready to use, they are not part of a routine vocabulary. They are enchantments, spells that force you reflect and ponder on the life passing by you. Serendipity. Things been brought together by a reason. When I think back, this moment is the definition of serendipity. It tasted like a knowledge that I always had, a buried piece of information from a distant place, indulging in making me feel stupid, naïve, appearing at the edge of the moment to show its ugly face, and say to my face "you knew, you always knew, but you didn't see". For how long did I knew?

"How long did they know? About me and the rest?" I knew the answer. Why was I even asking it? Since I first remembered. Since the very beginning I supposed. No, I knew.

"A few weeks ago, Dia" Carrie tossed that. "Since you went back to work. They were looking for you for months. But I found you. I took care of you and brought you to health. Mal and I, we both did. But she didn't know, she is innocent. She has nothing to do with all that" Her sentences were slowly not making sense anymore. She paused and sat down, weary. "If you have to blame someone, it's me you should blame"

I was blaming her.

"So everything that Chris said about you..."

"It's true" She replied. "They offered to help. To try and merge the information they had with ours. Maybe we could find more about what happened, what was the cause of the accident. It was an interesting idea. Perhaps we would be able to know more, who knows? But I said no. I did not trust it" She stood up, tired, still a heavy burden on her shoulders. "And then your friend arrived and told you all that. Out of nowhere, he comes back with all that information. Isn't that suspicious too?"

"What are you suggesting?" I felt cornered.

"I'm suggesting Dia, that you should open your eyes and see what's happening. Why did he come back? Just to see his father and to see you? Exactly the week that you returned to the office? Are you going to stand here and tell me that this is not at least a very fortuitous accident?" Carrie knew how to argue, and she also didn't like to lose. And yes, those were serendipitous happenings, but everything he said was true, and everything I knew about Carrie was not.

We talked for hours. I shouted at her, called her names, called her a traitor, usurper, malicious, words that I have never used before. She received them quietly. I asked if she knew about my mom, she said "yes". About the foundation, about the accident. "Yes" and "yes". There wasn't much more to be said. I accused her; she refracted the accusation. I knew it wasn't easy for her, but it was fucking hard for me too. And because of that I was more cruel than necessary.

"You drugged me with those mints. You weren't trying to help me recover my memories at all, you were lying to me. Fuck! I trusted you. You know that?" I cried that.

I threw the tin can of mints at my room's door. "Fuck you!" came out as a kitten trying to roar, pathetic and childish, but I wanted to make sure she understood.

We stood in that moment, a thick moment, it held us both there, staring at each other, waiting for anything to end that. I ended that. I opened the door of my bedroom and thought. How much Carrie helped me, how much she had supported me, and those thoughts held the door, just a little longer. And then I slammed door shut.

I broke down inside. I cried, siting by the door. I wanted to punch the floor, to punch it so hard I could hide inside the hole I created in the floor. I wanted to live inside that crater. The crater was consuming all the things around me. First mom, then Chris, now Carrie. The moonlight lit the room, a dreaded light, a sad, angry, betrayed light.

I locked the door, fell on the bed, and thought of

how I lost things I didn't even know I had.

I was told that my mother was an artist, a masterful creator, making beautiful trinkets, jewels, and paraphernalia. I remember the smell of the workshop, of metal and wood. That was a lie.

I was told that she made blades and knives, that she loved that. That she was a beloved blacksmith. Her knives had a certain devir, a presence, a type of magic you could not see, but feel. Like the blade could cut through flesh, but also through tissues invisible to the human eye. That was a lie.

I was told she experimented with metals and alloys, natural and man-made alike. She was one of the very few.

I was told that the foundation was more than a technology and research institution. They were trailblazers, rule bending, cutting edge. Their gaze was not to be bound to the confines of our earth. No, their sight was aimed to the skies, beyond the ventured space, beyond humanity's small voyages to our kind and gleaming satellite. Beyond the boundaries of technology.

I was told that they have ventured far into our system and found particles of an essential aspect of universal law. An aspect that both promotes our very existence and limits our unbounded movement. Gravity.

I was told they split, removed, reconfigured, and remodelled that particle, and made a metal out of it. A metal infused with the essence of that particle, of that character, of the rules of the universe. Gravitonium.

I was told that she worked and bound with that metal. But that did not play as expected. That my mother, feeling the immense force contained within it, sought to hide its existence. I did not know when my mother left. I did not know that the metal caused the scintillance.

I was told all that. And that she was alive.

***

ON RECOLLECTION

It was late when I decided I couldn't stay longer. I packed what I could pack, and left things I shouldn't have left. I did not bother to keep quiet or to make my exit any stealthier than it needed to be. It was a decision and not a reaction. I wanted to keep thinking that, even though the whiplash was so strong, neckbreakingly strong. I left through the front door, with all the lights out, all but the faint light coming from the kitchen door. I knew she was there, watching, waiting for me to turn around and look back, to lose my feet, to drop my bags and regret my decision. I did not.

By the door, I stopped. It would be the last weight to be left behind. I tossed my tin can, rattling with all the mints inside, onto the side table. Not with anger, not with displeasure, not even with disgust, only satisfaction to show that I did not need it. I knew I still did, but symbols are stronger than the actual thing, the actual act, and so, it symbolised my own loss.

I forced myself not to turn and forced my pad on

the panel. It buzzed and unlocked the door. It was suddenly dark.

But the moonlight illuminated the town below, refracting through the air above the crater, and hitting the glass windows of the foundation, and reflecting all the city lights. It looked almost alive at night, tiny artificial fireflies.

My pad rang once. A message.

Chris and I exchanged pad digits when we met, and I promised I'd let him know if I needed anything after tonight. Tonight, when I confronted Carrie, tonight, when I left the only home, I could remember. Tonight, a night of open skies and fireflies, the message read "I'm waiting for you by the bakery".

For a few minutes I just stood by the roadside, watching the town move. He asked me if I remembered his gran's bakery. I did not. I pushed and tried to squeeze it out, but luckless. We were younger, children, playing with dough and flour, thinking we were helping make bread. I said I remembered; I don't know why. I wanted to remember, I wanted to feel those memories again. But there were not there.

I typed, sent, and went my way down the road. The late night was almost turning into early morning when I reached the bakery. The only light in the sparsely lit turn into the alleyway, and the faint silhouette I saw, seated by himself, I knew belonged to Chris.

"Hey", I said quietly.

He looked up, eyes red from waking up, pulled from mid dream perhaps. "Oh, hi...Dia. Did you...?"

I closed my eyes and nodded, pointing to my backpack and the duffel bag stripe crossing over my shoulder and over my chest.

"Are you okay?", he asked, standing up, trying to grab one of the bags. I resisted.

"I'm fine. I don't know if it was the best decision", I was sure it was not a good decision, but it might have been the only one. "I just did. I couldn't stay there".

Chris crossed his arms, shifting on one leg, then on the other, acting tense, uneasy. "And did she tell you everything? That she told the foundation, that she..."

I raised my hand, asking him to stop.

"Do you remember anything else?", I asked. What was I looking for there?

"Remember...remember what?", he asked visibly confused.

"Anything. Something like the time we played in

the bakery. I want to remember something else", I asked one more time.

"Oh, right...I see...do you want to come in?", he said, pointing through the open door, into the brightness inside.

"No, I can't", I dismissed his question quickly. "Tell me something from when we were small. Something we have done together, a place we've been, a stupid thing we've done"

He looked puzzled, maybe unhappy of how I reacted to his invite. "I...I don't know Dia, there were so many things", his hands held the back of his neck, as he paced in front of the open door.

"Just one thing, only one. I want to have just another memory from us", I said anxiously.

He stopped and looked at me, eyes trying to find mine, moving fast, in thinking mode. "Well...there was this one time, right after...this", he pointed to the scar on his face, "we were having a break from one of your mum's classes. Dad was there too, they were talking inside, and didn't want us to hear them arguing", he raised a finger, asking me to wait. And I did.

He ran inside, disappearing on a left turn, coming back less than a minute later, and with two chairs on his hand. The chairs were supposed to be familiar, I should have remembered them, sitting there with him, with his grandad, at the bakery. But nothing. They were simple, meaningless chairs for me.

I sat, and he jolted back inside. This time, he came back carrying of almost warm coffee and the creamy, caramelized tart. The smell of that did remind of something. But not memories. It simply made me think of Chris again.

"Grandpa made them earlier, they should be good still. Of course, they're not as good as when we would steal them right out of the oven, but they're still tasty", he said laughing, expecting me to follow. I wished I could, so I pushed a chuckle, more of pity than joy. More of pity of myself than anything else. "And the coffee was seating there in the coffeemaker, heating up...only the best", and he smiled broadly.

"Thanks, looks very tasty", I bit the edge of the still crisp, flaky dough, letting some of the cream spill on my lap. I giggled, of a happiness I forgot I had in me, and was looking to find it again.

"So", I said, mouth still full.

"Ah yeah, the story", Chris cleared his throat with a loud cough, as if he were ready to perform, "I think that was the day Dad told your mum that we would be going away. Maybe that's why this memory still sticks to me. It was one of the last times we've seen each other", he took a sip of the coffee, and swallow before carrying on.

"We were sat by the river, in front of your place, right below that dry tree, do you remember?", he expected me to say something, but I could only shrug, and ask him to keep going, "right. We were watching the fishes go about. They were following the flow of the river, going down towards the vale, and then dropping at the falls, where they would lay their eggs. Anyway, there were a few of those small fishes. They were so small; we were a little surprise on how they weren't eaten yet by the large ones. But more than that, they were swimming against the river", Chris looked at me, again, waiting for a reaction.

"Well, we kept looking at them, seeing when they would just give up and let the river take them all. And one by one, all the tiny fish lost their strength, stopped fighting, and were dragged by the current. All but one. It kept swimming, kept fighting, kept pushing up. That one tiny fish, against the whole river. We were watching it, cheering, trying to push along with it. But it just couldn't, and it let go. And you", he pushed the air from his mouth, spitting bits of flaky tart, and laughed, "You silly girl, dropped into the river, headfirst", he made a sound that it should be that of water splashing, "I started running after you, trying to help you, but the river was going too fast. After the turn, I lost you, and couldn't see you anymore, so I took the shortcut through the woods, and when I came out the other way, you were trying to climb back, holding on a branch", he kept smiling the whole time he told the story. I was listening so eager, eating the words more than the tart, drinking it all more than a river of coffee.

"You managed to roll back up, using only one hand. Do you know why?", I swung my head, "Because on your other hand, you were holding the tiny fish. You kneeled on the mud, opened both hands, and it was there, a small, brilliant dash of blue, trying to breath. The water you should have swallowed, you kept in your mouth, and spat it out on your hands. You rushed past me; I couldn't even ask if you were okay. I just heard you saying, 'I have to save it'. And you did". Chris looked proud, fulfilled.

"I jumped", I finally said, without taking my eyes from his. "I didn't fall. I jumped"

"Maybe", he dismissed. "But that was pretty funny"

"Blue", I murmured, without thinking.

"Yeah, you called it Blue. It had a line of blue, looked almost like light", Chris said, almost falling from the chair. "Did you remember, Dia?"

"I don't know", I drank the last of the coffee. "And after that?"

The night was getting colder, a breeze strolled by both of us. Chris sighed deeply. "After that, me, dad, and my mum went to the Capital. It was fine for a while, until dad…", the sentence was left unfinished. No one needed to finish it. He sniffed and spoke. "Are you coming in or not?"

"No, not now", I answered. Maybe I should have stayed, maybe I should have been there earlier. "I'm staying at a friend of mine. I need to go actually; she must be waiting for me to come"

He stood, cleaning his clothes from the crumbs. "Are you sure? We can keep talking, I can keep telling you things we've done. Do you remember that other time…?"

"No Chris! I don't fucking remember, okay? I don't remember anything. Is just a fucking mess in my head right now", I snapped at him. Why did I have to be like that? "Sorry. I just can't have more, not right now", I tried my best to smile. "Maybe some other time"

Resolute, he nodded and smiled back. "I'll pad you"

"Yeah, you do that", I said, grabbing my things and walking off.

***

ON DECISIONS

Dreamless nights have been common recently. The past week, my nights have been without any stories. No images, no lights, no interpretation of symbols, no nothing. I didn't know what was causing that. I have been without the mints, under a different roof, sleeping on a couch I could barely fit. Mal tried to make it as comfortable as possible, and I made it difficult for myself to rest. I tried to avoid talking, but with Mal there is no such thing as not talking. And even though I have begun to learn how to talk about nothing with her, it still made me anxious and uneasy. It was my fault mostly.

"Good morning Dia" Mal knocked at the door frame of her own living room, as to ask for permission to come in. "Did you sleep okay today hon?"

"No Mal, I haven't. My head is bursting open" I was missing the mints. Maybe that was a reaction, withdrawal from the comfort of the dream of memories.

"Oh, I'm sorry. Do you want something to eat

maybe? Some tea?" She crouched down, so to be at eye level with me.

I opened one eye and replied "Coffee?" And closed it back, as the light stung.

"Coffee, yes, of course. Silly of me, I forgot you prefer coffee. That's fine. That can be arranged, that can definitely be arranged, you do not worry" She hopped back to the kitchen.

I was still getting used to Mal's, and she to myself. But I could not thank her enough, ever, for opening the door and let me crash on her couch that morning. And since then, I have reconsidered everything I had done. Since I woke up, since Carrie found me, since going back to work, and then Chris. All that were tossing and turning inside my brain, as if I could somehow change the solution, change the outcome. I couldn't. I couldn't even remember my mom's face and the last time I had seen my friend.

I haven't heard from Chris since…since that day we met. I expected him to maybe come looking for me, or to try and get in touch, tell more of what he knew. But he disappeared, just like a mirage when you get too close and too thirsty. Maybe he was also trying to avoid Carrie. If all that he told me was true – and every day I hoped it was, otherwise, I had done one fucking huge mistake – I couldn't blame him. I cut connections with her. I left, without a note, without a goodbye. But I left believing I could find the answers I was looking for.

Everything was fitting so well. I went back to the office, Chris came back to town, and then I left Carrie just I was reaching some sort of breakthrough. Maybe too well.

I heard Mal shouting from the kitchen. It burnt my ears, and I could only say, in a suffered loud moan "Black Mal...just black"

She joined me soon after, with a tray full of biscuits, her tea, and a cup of very watery coffee. "Sorry Dia, I'm not very good with coffee. I don't actually like it very much. I hope it's okay" I sipped the steaming liquid, and shivers crawled up my back and the back of my tongue. I closed my eyes, and I tasted all the tastes. "Is it good?" Mal asked.

"Yeah...it's...it's good" I garbled a few words, trying not to pass out. "Thanks"

"Oh that's great. Great" She happily sip her own tea and grabbed a butter biscuit. She cracked that in half, by the seam, and handed me one of the halves, and before I could refuse, she said "From where I come from, those biscuits are for sharing" I took it, for traditions sake.

Through sounds of sipping and chewing, Mal asked. "Do you want to talk? About anything? Is fine if you want, you can tell me. But if you don't, it's fine too, I don't mind. Whatever you prefer, okay? I just want to make sure you know that this is a safe space and that there's nothing you cannot tell me hon"

"Did you know? About Carrie?" She went numb, still. For a moment I wondered if I had even asked the question. "Mal, did you?"

She pierced her lips and swallow dry and put her tea and the last bit of the biscuit down. "I'm sorry hon, I should have noticed. I really should have. I was there, with you and her when she found you. Oh, I should have noticed. I am so sorry you had to go through this" She pulled her handkerchief out and cleaned the tears forming in her eyes. "No, I didn't know Dia. Not because it was hidden, or because Ca...she was keeping it secret, but because I didn't press, and didn't push her to let me help more" She grabbed my hands, which were still holding the coffee mug. "Do you forgive me Dia?"

What could I say? She saved me once when I first woke up and then now, she gave me a roof and a couch to crash. "Of course I do Mal. Sh...F... Yes, I forgive you. There's nothing to forgive, don't worry" She smiled and caught the tears falling down her cheeks.

I put the mug down, and told her "I have to go to the office Mal. I have to find more about me, about things I've been told, about Chris too" I let that simmer between us. "I have to"

"Yes hon, you do. And you will always have a fort here, you know right?" Mal said gently.

"I do"

***

I loved how the light breaking through the windows of the old church. It becomes quite warm after midday, and less aggressive and intrusive than the morning light. An intriguing orange hue built up in the room, mixed with the reds and blues and yellows of the windows, a warm aurora. I thought of the people that built that old church. Would they have felt this warmth too? Or was this place in a completely different weather system? What was their plan when creating this building? Would they also be thinking of myself thinking of them? Which kind of deity was reverenced here, which kinds of rituals, which types of dogmas and writings would leave this place to prey and to pray on others, which types of taboos would be kept inside, hidden, touching and untouched? This religion was pompous, for gold and myrrh had their place within the rites and the tribunes of celebrants. We knew that there were statues, frescos, reliefs, images of their gods, their patrons. And the gods, were their benevolent and givers, or destructive and possessive? It is not the god that befits evil, but the ones who build monuments to them. Gods do not need to beguile the ants, they are indistinct from the ants themselves, for they neither remain nor survive, but are.

I awed and sighed at the display of lights and colours for a long time. Seating down by my work-station, with the smell of paint and wood, and my head still hurting, I haven't noticed the glass door being activated, and moving. Vóra gently walked through, the only sound the door closing with a silent thump. "I thought I would find you here"

It took me more than I wanted to admit remembering who she was. Bad with faces, bad with names. Maybe I was simply bad with people. I dug deep looking for the friendliest greeting, which for all intent and purpose, I did not.

"ahn, hi. You are...Adonis's sister, right?" I half said that.

"Of course I am" She grunted "Or have you forgotten already, Dia?" My name came out crawling from her lips.

She sat down and stared at me. I felt seen. "I need to talk to you. It's about your dreams"

I have lost any sense of ground. The floor was gone, and I was falling. For a second or a generation I fell and found myself staring at myself, in the ceiling, looking back at me down at the ground. She was looking down at an empty body, a body falling. For a moment maybe there was the choice of staying like that, broken, separated. But her voice brought me back down.

"Did you hear what I said?"

"My dreams?" I said in instinct more than thought. Came as an animal cry more than human language. "How do you know about it?"

"How do we...fuck...right, Adonis told me to come and grab you, because we know that you have those...dreams of memories...fucking silly name...just like he does. But his' are less precise, less full. So we need you. He told me about you, and about your friend Carrie too" Hearing Carrie's name from someone else's mouth was not the most pleasant thing. "And that other friend of yours, I don't know his name"

"Chris?" I answered.

"Whatever, can you come now, we need to talk, the four of us" She stood up and nodded to the door, to the hallway, to the complex.

The taste of iron, of ginseng, maybe liquorice and mint. All the questions I had at the moment were just stupid and useless. How did she know? Her brother told her. How much did she know? As much as I did perhaps, maybe a little more. For how long? Did it even matter?

***

ON THINGS LEARNED

I f felt so alien to walk through those corridors. Streamlines of wiring and metal, a track only broken by a smooth glass door every ten odd steps. I imagined feeling claustrophobic just thinking of walking through those aisles, but it seemed less so there.

I kept following the woman in front of me. Her steps were precise and decisive, only disturbed by the slight limp on her left hip. Every few steps, she needed to readjust her pace, so she would wobble, however graceful that would look, her shoulder-length, fine and thin, jet black hair would bounce to her right as her right left received the limp. Nothing major, imperceptible even, in any other circumstance. But I was nervous, I was feeling my stomach take a will of its own, and perform somersaults in my belly, and for that I needed to have a point to focus my attention. The corridors continued as they started, no sign of a change of scenery anytime soon, so I choose to find an undetectable flaw in the only thing moving and alive in front of me, and try to make sense of the whole movement, its idiosyncrasies, its flow. Step, limp, hip, shoulder, hair, wobble, and begin again.

She didn't say a word since we crossed the door that separates the old building from the new. Her intent was strong, and vague. She didn't tell me what was happening, other than she was taking me to speak with her brother, the other person who was having dreams about the scintillance, who was talking with my best friend, behind my back, and that now apparently was also seeing myself in his dreams. If I struggled to understand the circumstances that brought me to that stage in time, in space, and in feelings, I wasn't confused enough.

"Vóra?" I had to break that silence. Me, breaking a silence.

"Yes" Just yes. A flat, unemotional, almost unintentional "yes".

"Where are we going?"

"We are going to talk with my brother about his dreams. He said you know about that too. About strange dreams. Dreams that happened" As elusive as our whole interaction to this point.

"Yeah, I think so. I have been having those dreams since" my memory was still hidden by a thick fog, a fog of light, of Carrie, and of my mother. "Since the scintillance I imagine. I don't remember much about what happened"

"You don't remember? Can you see it in your dreams? Your memories?"

"I can. Sometimes. I can see images, symbols almost, like a cryptic message that needs to be solved by finding the hidden pieces of information you are given"

"Homomorphic encryption" she spitted.

"Excuse me?" She didn't even flinch saying those words. I believed that those were indeed words.

She turned right on a crossroad of tunnels, I tried to keep up.

"Homomorphic encryption. It is a mathematical theory"

"Okay. I still don't know what that means" She stopped in front of one of the glass doors and picked up her pad to open it up.

"It's a theory that says that a mathematical function can be stored – or exists – in different shapes and basic forms. I don't know how to explain that to you. Do you know anything about math theory?" Her pad opened the door, and she got in without letting me finish my reply.

"No, I don't know any maths theory. I'm an anthropologist, we don't do maths, much"

"Great"

The laboratory was small, but the window facing the east side of the building let a flimsy light squirm in, through the half-opened blackout flap curtains. Vóra sat at her desk, looked at the blocked rays of light, and sighed loudly. "Okay, imagine you have a puzzle with the image of a house, by the river, and a tree" Awfully specific. "You can assemble and disassemble the puzzle following the cut-outs on the cardboard, correct?"

"Yes, of course"

"Okay. Now imagine that instead, you could separate the house from that image, and store it as its own entity. That is our theory of homomorphic encryption"

"And how that has anything to do with the dreams?"

She turned her chair, took her glasses and chuck them on her desk. Frustration perhaps, maybe something else.

"It means Dia, that those memories are pieces of a puzzle, but they are stored in different places. Parts are in your head, parts are in my brother's, others we don't know yet, maybe in someone else's dreams, maybe lost. We don't know for sure. That's why we need you, and you need us too" She turned her station on and close the window. The only light was the small skyline of blinking lights around us "Take a sit, Adonis will be right back"

I liked the natural light more than I thought before I entered that room. There was a different kind of life there. A rhythmic, pulsating life. Vóra's monitor was showing tables and sheets, and processes being completed, and started again, that I didn't want to understand.

"How do you organise your dreams?" her face and her hair were almost art in that light, with the reflections from the flickering light, the monitors chirping and humming, it was an unnatural beauty that half hypnotised me.

"Organise them? I don't...organise them. I have them, and then I remember, think about, try to figure out what they're trying to tell" At first, I thought I was the only one having memory dreams, or whatever she'd said they called it. Now, not only there are more than one, but those people also knew much more about them than I do. I mix of awkwardness and jealousy hit the back of my throat. "How about you? Do you write them down?"

She laughed. Not a loud laugh, but a surprised one. Even herself seemed shocked by her reaction. Vóra continued typing and snorted a smile directly at my pride. "No, we don't write them down. We record them, then we analyse the patterns against past dreams, looking for any homomorphism" As soon as she said that word, she turned, with a smirk "You know, the puzzle pieces?"

I was being pushed. I tried to push back.

"Well, apparently you didn't find much, since we need the help of an idiot that doesn't even know math theory"

"Look, I'm not trying to be your friend right now. And we do need you" She sounded more serene, defeated even. "We have been trying to find as much as we can, but we ran out of the mints, been months now. Without them, the dreams are extra disorganised. They are unruly, the information runs away, it is flaky sometimes, pudding-like other times. We try and grab them, just so they ooze out through our fingers"

"Mints? Do you know how to get them?" I haven't been thinking about them for so long, that if feels very strange to be feeling so eager. What I wanted to say was that I knew what mints meant, that I used to be close to someone who had knowledge on how to get it, but I myself didn't have any with me.

"Yeah, the same place you had yours I imagine. The lady you used to live with, Carrie, she works for the foundation too" She didn't look at me while she was typing. "Those things are for higher ups only, people in charge of things. They're still in testing, they say. They make your brain fuzzy when you go to sleep, and creates a mind tracking system, so they know the location of everyone working for them at any time, all the time"

My heart dropped and broke as a crystal in million pieces.

"You didn't know" Her voice was almost caring, almost worried. "Look, I don't know what you had with her, or if you were together. But whatever she said about that, she was lying to you. Adonis knew her. He's been having meetings with her for a while, all until last summer, when she decided to cut relations, and closed her doors to him...so we ran out of the mints"

My face was just a blank canvas, empty, without action, movement, or insight.

"Ah there he is" She said standing up and touching my shoulder quickly and went outside. Pin and needles, crawling under my skin, waking my limbs, my organs, my faceless façade.

"Vóra, did you find her?" their voices seemed distant from the corridor. I just mounted my will to turn in the chair and stare into the illuminated rectangle, and the two half silhouettes talking. I was forcing myself to listen, trying to hear things I think I wasn't prepared for.

"Yeah, she's there. She's a little shook up after what

I told her. But she'll be fine. I hope so. Do you have the plans for the…?"

"Here. I, ahn…will show you inside. Better this way"

"Alright, I'll go to the restroom. Go talk to her"

"Shit…right"

The murmurs stopped, and one of the shadows came in, taking the form, the texture, and the shape of the one called Adonis. The third time I met him, the first time he would meet me.

"Hi. How are you? Is, ahn…is everything okay?" He asked as if I was a toddler, expecting me to say I was hungry, or sleepy, or bored. I actually was, all of that.

"I'm okay. I'm confused" I said, looking down at my feet "Your sister" I scanned the door quickly, just to be absolutely sure she wasn't listening. She terrified me. "She told me about you. That you have dreams too"

He sat down in front of me, took his hat and gloves, and proceed to stare at his hands, folded on his lap. "Ahn, yes…I guess everyone has dreams right?" He waited for my reaction. Was he expecting me to laugh maybe? "Sorry. Yes, yes. I do have the dreams of memory. I see things, things I cannot remember, but I know that they are my memories"

"She also said something about a theory, and puzzles, I didn't get any of that shit" I told him.

"Yes!" He said loudly, turning from one side to the other, trying to find something. He grabbed the notepad right behind me, on the other desk. "Homomorphic encryption. We are trying to run models of the small pieces of the images I see in my dreams and working on the assumption that they do not necessarily tell a linear story but are scrambled fragments of ideas."

He continued talking and explained mathematical behaviours, m-theory, holography, things I have heard or knew existed, and that was it. He was excited, happy, joyful, explaining incomprehensible and fantastic things. For me, those moments could have come directly from a fantasy book, and I wouldn't notice the difference. But I was paying attention, so much attention. Not on the words. But on him. His eyes glimmering, his hand in an agitated dance, papers flying and falling like snow in a cold dark evening. So much passion and so much knowledge.

I haven't noticed at first. My face became fresh, my eyes heavy, my mind full of ressentiment maybe, for sure anger, and confusion would turn that mix into an explosive combination. My hands and feet, I lost all the feeling on them. And I cried.

"What happened? What...what did I say?"

I didn't want to cry. Not in front of someone I didn't know.

"I need to find it" The silent in the room was paste, it was peanut butter. Heavy, sticky, damp.

"What? What you need to find?"

"I need to find who I am" I lifted my head, and our eye met. I have again noticed his eyes. From far away they could be black, or a generic dark shade. But up close, they were grey. A metal grey, beaten and folded iron. "Adonis, I need to find who I am. I don't know what we are going to do, or how we are doing it, but I want to do it too. I need to. For myself, for my mother. For my memories and the memory of the people that are gone. I want to see my mother Adonis. Will you help me?"

Sometimes we stop controlling parts of our bodies. Limbs, organs, senses, they flare up and take a conscience and an agency of themselves. They disregard the human in the brain hierarchy and, revolt, they are now independent, acting with free will and free movement. A life revolution.

My hands held his hands, so tightly, his fingertips were becoming pink, then red, and were moving to blue and purple. I was looking inside of his eyes now, and he didn't look away this time.

"Yes" and he broke the spell. "Yes, I will help you"

I blinked and gained control of my body again.

Brought my hands back to me, let him be.

"Sorry" and "thank you" was what I said.

We both took deep breaths.

"Hey, you both" Vóra knocked on the open door. "Come on, she's here"

I looked back at Adonis. For some reason, he was a safe haven in this place.

"It's okay. Doctor Anansi knows about it all. She is helping us with all this. Come" he extended his hand to me. "She will help us"

***

Doctor Anansi. She was known in the foundation as one of the most important contributors to the renaissance of the ARIA foundation after the incident. She, and a handful of others, were given the task to reconstruct not only the 5-mile radius of destructions caused by the scintillance, but also to rebuild the trust and confidence the town had on them. Most thought that after the foundation bought the University and created their selection program, they have started to burn bridges in town. And then the scintillance happened, within the foundation plants. No one would believe that six months later, they would even still exist.

But they did, they continued, and they flourish. The amount of work that those few employees put into saving their workplace and to rebuild the city around it, was unimaginable. Mere weeks after the city centre and the university campus were flattened, they had already put-up temporary sites and mobile offices and laboratories. People were impressed by their incredible work, but also, they started to flock around the foundation for their impetus and charity. Around the main institution, many others were founded, aiming to rescue and give opportunities for those who have lost anything for the scintillance. Their heart, their blood, and their resources were aimed at the town, and at the people. And because of that, the first fully restored entity was belief and trust.

And amongst such employees, Doctor Anansi Delaqua was the most visible and most present. She used to coordinate and run the donation and charity programs herself. She walked amidst the people. Everyone knew her, and consequently, they felt they knew the foundation itself. She was the face of the corporation, and everyone loved her.

I saw her a few years ago, in a talk at the start of term lecture. She talked about research, about the technologies they were developing at the Engineering department, and how that would boost the possibility for a new era of space travel. One day, she used to say, we would walk again on the steps of our forefathers, and we will meet them in the future. It was supposed to be a beautiful and impactful phrase, but I remembered thinking that it was nonsense and contradictory. The future would meet the past. Bullshit. But I couldn't help myself been fascinated by her energy, her passion, and her determination.

She signed a copy of her book and asked my name and what I was studying. "Anthropology", I said, expecting her to brush that aside, and dismiss me with a nod and a smile. "Is that so?", she replied surprised, "I graduated in Anthropology too. I was always interested in people and how they see the world differently from myself". She handed the book and looked at me, gave me a kind smile, and proceeded to talk to the next person in line. It was not until I got back home and started reading the book that I noticed the inscription in the first page of the book: "to understand the universe, we need to use the tools of mathematics and physics we learn in life. To understand people, one needs to live a thousand lives, and look at a thousand universes. Good luck". I wondered what that meant. I wondered if she would remember.

***

Another set of labyrinths of corridors, and glass doors leading to other offices and laboratories, dim, blinking lights. This area of the building was as aseptic as the ideas Vóra and Adonis were trying to input in my head. Straight lines, shapeless walls, no uselessness of decorations. The entire time walking behind the two siblings, trying to keep up but also looking and internalising that environment. My idea of decoration is not as explosive and visible as others'. I had mostly my books, my games, and my music as pieces of aesthetic flavours. I liked to show what I liked, or who I was, very sparse and moderately. Going into my room...my old room, at Carrie's, was like stepping through a threshold into a world of fantasy, but in reverse. The adventures in the magic land were always fascinating and exciting, but the final return to the familiar and quiet was a deserved rest. I enjoyed having an uncluttered space, minimal and functional.

However, this was beyond what I would even find comfortable, familiar, or desirable. In a way it has made me aware that by seeking the things I have lost – or taken from me – every step of the way was going to bring me to a new and unfamiliar setting. And that made me extra attentive, extra focused, and prepared for the next step.

Doctor Anansi's office was nothing if unexpected, given where I had just come from. Beige walls in need of a full repaint, bookshelves of all sizes, styles, materials, and age, holding books of an even more extensive gradient of existence. A white and black plywood, more modern, apparently recently added to the room, and an older version of the same desk, this in a more dire state. Like a politician finishing a mandate and being swapped by one of the same qualities, of fake wood and cheap making. The desks were put in front of each other, making a larger surface, as to be a platform for blueprints, stellar maps, and coding in piles of paper. The room was backed by a massive window, looking down at the green in front of the old church, and further on to the woods that staple the edge of town.

In front of that view, an old, heavy, scared, and dark mahogany wood, finished with carved panels, depicting flowers and leaves, which probably didn't exist anymore, and brass, adorned handles, turned dark green or grey. The green and white marble top was barely visible under the writing apparel, the keyboard and computer, and the coffee cup and press in the metal tray. Desks such as that one was not only incredibly looking, but also rare, and mostly seen in books or the history museum. That piece of furniture would make anyone drool in desire and wonder how one would have shown up in a space like that. It took me a moment to realise that I had been there before. Years ago, a life ago. But it was indeed a place I have visited before, when I was younger perhaps. The actual memory was foggy and distrustful, but as unreliable as it was, I could feel I had been there.

The old church wasn't the only part of the old university that survived the scintillance. Behind it, its tall, single tower, almost due to miracle, but mostly due to the diligence of the foundation, was kept up and alive. It served, in the past, as the old art and craft antiquary, been held at the top room of the building. Below, due to the lack of windows, was used mainly as storage. After the renovation, it was kept as part of the north wing, even though it was still attached to the old church, and to what now was the office we were less than an hour ago. In the same way we normally didn't visited the north wing, the tower became out of bounds. Not before, as I visited as a child, and not then, at that very moment.

"Doctor" Vóra questioned loudly. We could not see anyone in the room. "Are you here?"

No answer. Only the silent hum behind us, and the raffle of paper inside, somewhere.

"Vóra? Is that you?" the bodyless voice spoke from above. Not godly or awe inducing, but quite earthly. "I'm here. Up here" And as soon the voice said that, a few sheets of wrinkled, already written on paper dropped suddenly, or as sudden as paper can fall.

The three of us got in, looked back, and then up. Right above the door, a metal mezzanine surrounded the backside of the office, which was then backed by a whole other set of bookshelves, climbing all the way to the round ceiling. This place had more books than anywhere else I had been before. And in front of the books, the owner of the disembodied voice was trying to keep the rest of the sheets of paper under control. More of then dropped and fell, however.

She was quite different from the controlled, calm, and centred woman we all watched giving the livestream speech a few months ago, talking about the foundation's new space program. This person was...overwhelmed. The doctor climbed down the metal staircase, trying to hold her own balance, while more sheets of multicoloured paper and a notepad dropped on her feet, and almost made her trip and fall.

"Vóra" She drop her burden on her beautiful mahogany desk, and whit a heavy breath, she turned to the three of us, took of her glasses, and breathed out "can you please help me with that? There are a few more files in the archives up there. Grab the PR-24 and the SC-89 and bring them down. The whole thing, I'll sort them out when I'm done"

Adonis's sister simply nodded and decidedly climbed the stairs, two steps at a time, not showing any sing of struggling. I thought of her limp. Maybe I was imagining.

"Adonis" The Doctor said, taking us both from a trance, waiting to be summoned back to reality. "Do you want to introduce me to her please? And come over here, I need you to start the setup for the update I've made to the coordinates okay?"

"Ahn, yes, of course, ahn...this is..." I could not let him speak. I have been dragged, lied to, betrayed, contradicted for a while now. I have been told things, but not yet found out about them myself.

"I'm Dia" I said, stepping closer to her desk, and pushing Adonis to do whatever he needed to do. "I work at the office, right below us, and I have been brought here because they said you can help me. Help us."

Anansi put her glasses back, skewed her eyes and stood up. She could not be too much older than any of the three of us. Her dark, curly, thick hair framed her face. She was short, and her whole presence was so much taller than her body would reach. As I walked towards her, I could see that she was tired. Her eyes dark and concave, and a few bloodshot veins in her eyes were made abruptly larger because of the glasses.

"Dia, is that it?" Her voice was warm, loud, and low, a strange combination coming from her. "Okay, can you please get a chair and bring it over? They are there, behind the door, okay? Bring a couple more for the two of them" She pointed to the entrance door, and to the pile of foldable metal chairs stacked next to a loose pile of books. "I'm sorry, I got a little behind today, and I couldn't set the room. That's okay right?" She addressed the two siblings, who promptly made affirmative noises from where they were.

The doctor continued "I had a few meetings with the heads of department, including Anthropology" she looked and pointed at me when she mentioned my office "and we were deciding what to do about the projects. I said we should consider making a multi-area project, to gather all knowledge and ideas from different fields of study."

Adonis said from his seat "All done here. And ahn...what did they say?"

Vóra handed the professor a pile of files and archival envelopes "Well, they thought it could be an incredibly good idea, so they would have good word of mouth and promotion from all areas of the institution. I honestly thought they would fight for an enclosed project, but that looks to be the least of our problems now, right?" Vóra and Adonis agreed, and came to where Anansi was.

I set the chairs in front of her desk and sat in one of them. I choose the corner, expecting that the siblings would sit next to each other. "I'm sorry, can you tell me what's happening? Why am I here?" The three others stared at me, as if I were an intruder that had just manifested in the room, instead of an intruder brought in by them.

"Dia. Do you know what this place is?" the doctor sat on her desk, facing me down. I nodded and tried a guess.

"I don't know. I assume that this is part of the

engineering department" I was probably correct in assuming that, so I jumped to a conclusion which I knew I would be able to hit the landing.

"Yes, it is. And I am Anansi, and you have met Vóra and Adonis. They work with me" No surprises up to that point. "Now, that is quite obvious, and you would have guessed at least up to this point without any help, right?" Read my mind. I agreed with a shook of my shoulders. "Yes. From this point forward, the things you will hear and learn are less public. Much less. And for this communication to work, I will need to be sure that you are ready to receive it, and that you will be ready to keep that to yourself"

"I don't even know what this is all about. I don't know how anything you say will affect me" I was confused, but me deminer needed to be strong, so I stood my ground, and played a steady façade. "I think at this point I have the right to know what I'm going to be dragged into"

"Yes, you do" Anansi said. "But first, we will ask you a few things, and if we are happy with it, you will know what we know"

"What could I possibly know that you need?" I rebutted.

"We need to know what happened during the scintillance" the Doctor cross her arms and waited. "Tell me about your dreams of memory"

***

A few hours later, myself and Adonis left the compound. I wouldn't be able to leave by myself. Vóra and the Doctor stayed back. We walked the whole journey back outside without exchanging a single word. I could feel he wanted to say something, but I said more than enough, more than I could, about things I didn't remember, and about things I didn't even know had passed.

They asked me about the scintillance, as if I could recall, as if I could remember anything. I told them about my dreams, my mother, the symbols, about Carrie and how we were trying to recover those memories. About the mints, about our fight, about how I was trying to find a way to discover what actually happened to me. I didn't talk about Chris, I thought it would be unnecessary to include another person in this circle, and for all intents, I would still have something that only I knew. I needed to have at least something on them.

Trust is a very strange concept. Trust comes exclusively from the person trusting, regardless of what the trustee does or how he or she behaves. It's a one-way street, and it relies on the trusting side to perceive what should be trusted. I trusted Carrie, and that failed. I was then in a position where I should have used any instinct or intelligence, I had to analyse the situation, and put my trust on those people, or to turn my back and do what I had to do myself. In that moment I could have both, so I took both. I trusted, and I didn't. One foot behind.

It was still bright outside. The clouds started to move and agglomerate, travelling from the hills up north, and folding, merging, getting darker and heavier. The sun was still alive, but the only sign of its presence was the silver linings, making lines and measures of the rainclouds above. A storm was forming, tonight was going to be loud, windy, and intense.

"Ahn, so, what do you think?" Adonis was standing next to me, hands in his pockets, slight long hair held back, a few loose locks floating in front of his eyes. "Do you want to go through with it?"

That was a question that I should have answered years ago, a lifetime ago. I spent the past six months trying to find my past, trying to find the truth, and have only been misled by the person who I trusted the most. Not only Carrie manipulated me for a reason that I still did not know, but she had also lied about her connection with the foundation. Then my oldest friend returned and brought me hope that one day we would find the truth, but that hadn't worked either, yet. Chris was radio silent for weeks, and I was hoping that he was still there, still with her.

And walking out of that room, I had more questions than answers. Things that I didn't even know existed, or things I could not imagine have been created. A lore that I have lived but did not remembered. But it was there. I could see it, as clear as the rainclouds forming above my head, I could see my memories. I could see Adonis's memories as well. The only two with the dreams. More time, they said, I would need more time to readjust the images and put them in an intelligible format. I was to go back again, to practice and to study. The first time I felt I was moving forward.

"Yes, I do" I said, a second later. "I want to see my memories the way you see yours too. I just…"

"What?" Adonis asked, turning his head smoothly.

"Do you trust it? Do you trust her?" I asked finally, it was killing me inside.

"I, ahn, think so. I don't have any reason not to. My sister does, and I trust her" He turned around, moving to go inside again. "I won't ask you to trust it, or to trust us. They have only showed what is inside your own head, a bit unscrambled. Whatever doctor Anansi is doing, she is doing for the good of people, for the good of science, and to find answers for our questions. We are working on this project for a long time, and we have had very little progress. But I know that with your help, we will be able to learn more about the scintillance, and about our past. It was through Doctor Anansi that I found my sister again" He waved his pad at the door panel, unlocking the door with a beep.

Adonis held the door a moment and said "Give it a chance. If it doesn't work. I will make sure you don't get to do it anymore"

I didn't answer. I just looked at him as he nodded and let the door go.

***

I walked alone back home, watching the afternoon turn into evening, the yellow becoming orange, then purple and blue. It was just when I got to the Balcony hills road, I realised that the up of the hill was not home anymore, and even then, I got there mechanically, automatically. It hurt for a second to turn around and walk the river road instead, to Mal's.

That night I spent awake. No dreams, no sleep, just my brain trying to figure what to do next. I watched the night pass considering my options. Either let those people look into my memories, and try to find more about myself, and consequently, more about the scintillance; or continue working alone, waiting for Chris to emerge again from whatever hole he was hiding, in the hopes he would bring a solution or a plan.

And that night I have decided to take my own plan. I would meet with Adonis and the others, and they would have their object of study. But I would have mine. Doctor Anansi's laboratory would be my own fieldwork. I would look, engage, learn, and let their ontology permeate my own ideas and premises. I would not be simply an object, I would perceive and analyse their ways of being, of thinking, and of communicating. I would become familiar with their tools, their techniques, and their environment.

I have not slept. I have watched the sunrise from my window. The clouds from the night before still lingered, heavy, above the town. They were moving slower now that the wind has settled and lost its breath. The rain always kept me awake. It was a good company for my awaken passage to the next morning. The last droplets were still falling when the sun broke the horizon line, and shattered the humid air with light, which then multiplied, reflecting and refracting into a million colours. A kind of poetry that I tried to achieve in life. That my mother found in metal and wood.

Mal had long left when I woke up. There was coffee in the coffee maker, and bread left on the living room table, for me probably. And before I could consider any other option, I grabbed the fluffy loaf and chugged the horrible watery coffee Mal tried to do again that morning. It did wake me up for sure.

I got used to walking horizontally, flat, towards the centre. Before I left Carrie's, from her flat, I could see the whole of the town. From the curve of the river in the west, to the woods and the rapids in the east; from the long stretch of hills up north, which climbed down to create a valley, to the balcony road, snaking down from the south hill, to encounter the markets, the shops, and finally, to alight by the green, and then the foundation. Everything was within my eyesight, and I could watch life goes by if I didn't want to participate in it.

Because I was not yet familiar with being at Mal's, I still would find myself lost and meandering through the uneven streets that would curve, and turn, and die on themselves again. An unplanned growth. The new development was only the initial project inside a much larger idea to merge with the next town. A sprawling, uneven root system, that connected nothing to nowhere. I took the river-bank route. A trail of dirt and rock that through time and use, was made into a path. The path was there before the new development, before the scintillance, before the foundation, even before me, and my mother, and her mother before her. That path was made by wandering feet and curious hands and eyes, that walked by the river for tracking, for water, and for food. A thousand steps, and a hundred thousand more, walking, building from one another, deliberately and viciously living by and for the river and its surroundings. A path that was made by craft, by communication, by perseverance, and by people. By permanence, by recollection, and by memory. I walked that path to recall and to recount the steps took before my own, I walked that path to create an event, to create a new memory.

No matter which path I took, however, all paths lead to the crater. And that day it took me past it, all the way to the front door of the old church, the building that I have been just the day before, that now seemed strange, foreign, alien.

The door beeped for my pad, and it opened itself as a reply. The mosaic of colours was even more dramatic than the rainbows outside.

***

ON BETRAYAL

Even with no lights, I could see the entirety of the office. The sun shone so bright, in the crisp morning. The windows ricocheted the light through all nooks and crannies, through all the desks, flipped chairs, open files, broken computers, and the sea of paper tossed, and stepped, and crunched, now dead on the floor. I ran to my station, wishing for that to be a dream. Not a memory dream, but a real, stupid, unreal dream, those ones that one awakes from and a few minutes later, doesn't even remembered what it was about.

It was not. It was as real as the dread I was feeling. I thought of many things to say, most of them empty curses and unanswerable questions. My books ripped apart and discarded as meaningless processed wood. My drawers opened, messed with, touched, and violated. My mug broken. My whole body shivered, trembled, and I started sweating. Who could've done that? And for what?

"Compose yourself", I said. I stood, scared, alone, but more than that, angry. The front door was locked. I went to the back door, behind the wash-room and the closets. Also locked, from the inside. No one came in, no one got out.

The only way into the office was through the glass door leading to the engineering wing. Whoever had violated my space, was still inside. Whoever had done that, was from the inside. It felt like a whole hour. I stood in front of that passage, un-willing and incapable of opening. A deep breath, another. I pulled my pad to unlock the mechanism.

A loud sound exploded in the room. Someone was moving towards me. I got distracted my own thoughts, and whatever was happening in the room behind me was gone. That was a mistake, how could I be so careless? Did someone shoot me? Was I hit? Why wasn't hurting? There was no blood. I dropped to the floor and pushed myself to the wall, backing myself in a corner, protected on three corners, with just one still unsafe.

There was no smoke, or shot, or weapon. Someone was coming from underneath the desk, pushing the fallen metal chair away.

"Oh my, Dia! Dia, is that you?" A sobbing, red, and panicking Mal came from beneath the surface, pushing furniture and electronics alike. "Oh Dia, hon! Oh, thank all the skies that is you. Oh no, no!" She dropped down, by my crouched legs, and held my hands on her sweaty, trebling palms.

"Mal" I finally uttered, in a midst of confusion and relief. "What happened here? Who did all this? Are you hurt, did they hurt you?" Mal was shook. I was shaking, too. Because of the ravage in my office, because of the unexpected, unearthed friend.

"No" Mal said amongst tears and snorts "No, I'm fine. I just…got scared. And then I hid under the desk. He didn't see me; I don't think he did. No, I'm pretty sure he didn't. Oh my, hon. He was knocking at the door, but more like smashing, punching than knocking. And I didn't answer, I thought I should at first, maybe someone had gone out and lost their pad, or their ID wasn't working. But I didn't, I didn't answer. I waited. And then it started again, but then it was stronger. And the punches were so angry, oh, so angry. And they stopped for a little bit. And I was waiting, just waiting. And I heard the doors from inside buzzing and beeping. And I was very scared. I just hid under the desk, and waited" She stopped to catch a breath "And I saw it all, hon. Everything"

"okay, and do you remember if he, she…" I questioned.

"He, it was a man" Mal replied, ready to continue her account, but I waved my hand in front of her and asked her to wait.

"Okay, he. Do you know who he was? Did he say anything? Can you remember his face?"

"I...I think I can, yes, yes, I can remember" She wiped her eyes and nose and held my hand while I pulled her up.

"Great" We walked back to the mess of papers and files. I picked the chair up and helped her sit. "Now, tell me what you remember"

"Okay, hon" She looked me in the eyes, holding my face in between her hands.

Mal cleaned her face with her handkerchief, swallow the last spec of cry, and cleaned her throat. "He came in from the door that goes to the engineering. He entered, I don't know how. Maybe he had a key, or a pad. Then he walked straight to your desk Dia. Straight! He started to check your papers and notes, and then the drawers, and files, then the computer. And oh my, he was getting angry, hon. He hit the desk and hit it again. He threw the papers, he stomped, and he stood there for a while, a minute maybe? A minute or two. Then he crouched down. Oh, I thought he would see me. I held my breath. He picked up a piece of paper and a pen and wrote something. I don't know what it was. I couldn't see. And then he left. He just left, left from where he came. Can you believe it?"

If that had happened a few weeks ago, maybe I wouldn't have believed her. But after the things I've learned and the people I met, maybe there was something more happening, something more than just my own memory and my own past. I tried to imagine a reason for someone to come and try to vandalize my things but couldn't. Not yet.

"You said he left a note" I pushed the chair towards my desk, and I rolled directly, almost, to my chest of drawers. Opened, desecrated. I moved the papers, picked up files, and tried to tide all my work back in their place. I still felt violated, watched even now, but the paranoia gave way to curiosity, so I kept looking instead of organising. I became the vandal for a moment. Under the mice, stuck underneath it. A folded piece of paper. I opened, and I couldn't read the text. I was more interested in the handwriting.

"Mal" I half said, "Did you see his face?"

"I did Dia. Oh hon" She almost started crying again "It was your friend, Chris"

***

Mal brought me a cup of coffee, as I finished talking about Chris. We spent an hour cleaning and organising our office. After we were done, we decided we couldn't stay there at all. We locked the doors, I took the note, and we walked to the café. 'I need to drink something' I remember saying, and Mal said coffee. I was thinking something more wine than that.

"Thanks" I murmured smelling the steam of the

coffee. It made my eyes burn and my forehead condensate. "Hm, that's good…I mean, not as good as yours", I smiled at her.

She smiled "That's fine hon. Are you okay? I don't want to push you to tell me anything else about it. Oh my, I didn't want to have to ask you about your friend, but given the situation, you understand that it was…" I held her hand and look straight at her.

"Mal, that's fine. I hate that it happened too. But you were there, and you needed to know" I smiled and proceed to drink my coffee.

"What you're going to do now Dia?" I didn't know. The note said to meet Chris, it said that he needed me, it said that he was close to find it.

"I'll have to go Mal. Thank you for the coffee, and for all. I will see you later" I meant that. I wanted to keep at least one friend, one person that I could trust. And if it couldn't be Chris anymore, that was fine. Maybe Mal, maybe someone else.

***

The night was cold, much colder than when it was raining. The sky was open, big, full of stars. All the heat was leaving the surface, going back to meet the coldness of space. I have waited until I was at home, safe, before I let Chris know I received his note. 'I'll tell you all', the message read.

I read and reread the note, as if a secret would be revealed if I kept staring at it. It didn't. It just got crumbled and ink began to fade away.

There was a choice in a piece of paper. How many memories I have shared and lived with Chris? He knew me more than many, more than most. And I, myself, didn't know enough about him anymore. I didn't know enough about myself. There was a choice, a choice that already made.

The memories from my mother, from my childhood were still so fragmented, so adrift in this sea of images, of dreams that don't make sense. She did teach us both how to work with metal. I could still feel the heat of the forge, the sparks of the hammer hitting the glowing blades, and the impact flowing through the anvil. I was good at it, mom used to say. I had a knack for it.

The only thing I still have from when she taught me. I haven't opened the box in so long. It still smelled of dry wood and old leather, and it weighed as much as it cost me to remember. She said one day she would make the best knife, the most beautiful, out of the best metal, to make a pair with my first. I kept that as a treasure, as a promise, and as a reminder. After a while, the promise went away, the reminder became vacant, and the treasure was a burden. Why couldn't I remember my own mother? Why was she lost? She was lost inside of me, lost in my memories, wondering aimlessly in my dreams.

My knife was crude, raw, visceral, unbalanced. I held it in my hand for the first time in years. I could see all the mistakes I had made. A slip in the chisel, too much pressure in the hammer, the blade was not straight, and the handle was still rough to the touch. I didn't know how to communicate with the materials, with my tools, with the techniques.

I looked and stared and measured that knife for a long time, so long in fact, that I had an after image of it in my retina. I could close my eyes and see it, there, right in front of me. My knife, my first mistakes, my first steps, my first errors and decisions. Decisions that moved and trailed my paths. I was always surprised by the things I did then. At that moment, that very second, I was deciding. Not what I was going to do, that was already decided. But I was deciding how to take the past, the memories, the stories, and the mistakes along with me to the path ahead. Fuck, I was being philosophical because of a knife. That one sharpened story of mine.

I fell asleep holding the unsheathed blade by my chest, feeling the cold blade caressing my skin, covering that deep scar. A dreamless night.

**

Chris was never in my dreams. The memory dreams. I saw my mom, I saw myself, and I saw others, but never Chris. His presence still lived in the still memories; the ones not shuffled by the scintillance. I remembered our child life, our plays, our growth, but those were not puzzled, those were there, visible, rewatchable, remembered, as a scar, by iron and fire.

He left before the incident that blew my brain into pieces, and because of that, the moments we have lived and experienced were intact, still alive in my mind. I knew him, as well and as deeply was I could possibly know myself, maybe even more, because my own memories were broken; maybe less, because I hoped that the Chris I knew was the same one I was going to meet. He had wrecked my office, looking for something that it did not belong to him, however. And because of that, I couldn't go alone, not now.

"I don't come to this side of town very often" Adonis said, both of us looking up at the top of the buildings. "Not anymore at least"

I stood and took it all in. The road up, the expectation, the things I would say, or do. "No, me neither" I joked, and then said. "Thanks for coming along. I don't know if I would be able to do this alone now. I'm losing people I can trust one after the other" I didn't say anymore. I couldn't burden him with something so heavy as trust.

Walking up the Balcony hills made my stomach-ache, and I felt my throat trying to swallow dry acid reflux. But we kept going. The top of the hill was my home, my safe space for so long, but then, it felt dangerous, strange, peculiar, other. An otherness that only develops and grows due to distance and time, and regret. And still, it was all other. I told myself I did not need to go all the way to the top, 'you're halfway there, you will turn right, and go to the flat, your home, and that's it', I said. The encouragement was less effective than I thought it would be, but I was not alone, and even if he was silent, he was there, and I thought that it was enough, at that moment it was enough.

The soft rain from the night before made the cobble slippery and unwieldy. As if ice was spread throughout the whole road, as a thin layer of invisible jam. It felt almost appropriate for me to have such a struggle to climb halfway through a stone street. It was the obstacle before the confrontation, a final test before the revelation of a major set piece. The home stretch was always the most difficult.

We walked up, slowly, and I was trying to think how I would react to seeing the two of them, together, in the same place. Each step was a monument to our story, each step was a bridge where the waters rushed and roared, and each step was a knife stabbed in my back. How did I end up here, like this? Every time an answer was given to me, millions of more questions arose, shadowing my horizon. All the edges of those steps, all sharp and cutting. I wanted to leave my blood behind me, drop my heart by the staircase. But climbing this crater was all heart, was all blood, cutting me feet, grinding my teeth, hands in fist.

I knocked. Once, twice. The voice inside was familiar, but I failed to recognise it, on purpose. I didn't let Adonis say anything either.

"Yes" he answered.

"It's me" I replied.

"Dia?" the other asked.

"Yes, it's me" unchanged, I again replied.

Locks and keys turning. The creek of the door was loud, raspy, almost human. A lament for the things about to happen.

Chris held the door open, forced a smile, and let me go in with a movement of his hand. I walked past him, a fury mixed with confusion and a tad of relief. I haven't heard from him for weeks. A multitude of thoughts rushed through my head.

"And who is this?" Chris asked, barring Adonis at the threshold.

"Can you let him in? He's with me" I came back, pushed Chris aside, and brought Adonis in. "Come Adonis, don't be standing there"

My eyes followed Chris' while I walked, my eyes like blades, like daggers ready to stab and kill. His sight was aimed at the other.

And quickly I saw her. Standing in front of me, with her pristine salmon suit. It had so much colour then, so much life.

"Dia, how are you? It's been so long" Hearing her voice was unreal as any of my memory dreams. Damp, noisy, disrupted, and broken. She said that as if she deserved. "Adonis, you as well?" she completed, almost unfazed by his sudden presence.

"How am I? I'm good Carrie. Thank you. I'm great. You know, I am very good. Because I was sad, I was horrified after I left the flat. I couldn't believe myself, that I could be so ungrateful, so egoist, so void of any feelings. I regretted, I cried, thinking that even though I was stabbed in the back, I still owned you. I did, I owned you my life, I owned you the opportunities you gave me, I owned you a lot. But I don't, not actually. You sold me a lie, you fed me a curtain, and I happily swallowed, because I trusted you. But I am good, I am better now. I learned and I am not so stupid" I forced those words, one by one, like a hammer nailing a window shut. "And still, even then, you didn't tell me all of it, did you?"

She seemed far, almost as she wasn't really there "No, Dia, I haven't. There is still so much you don't know, so much I kept from you, and so much I want to tell you" She walked towards me, pointed to the couch and the set coffee table. "Sit with me Dia, please" We both sit, and Carrie, seeing that Adonis was still standing, left her arm stand and her hand drop just enough as for him to understand that she wanted him seated as well.

There was a comfort in her voice. We had our more formal conversations by the window having coffee and tea. There wasn't the flat on top of the hill, there wasn't the majestic living room with the tall windows and patterned carpets, and there wasn't the home I knew.

Chris walked behind the couch and sat in the far end. He was quiet and restless, in a way that I didn't know him to be. Maybe all my memories were all compromised after all. Perhaps everything I thought I knew was not more than a product of some kind of elaborate brainwash through mint consumption, and I was nothing more than an empty vessel, a blank in which they have implanted fabricated reminiscences.

"Coffee?" Carrie offered, while she served herself her dark and aromatic tea.

"Do you know what those pills do?" I asked.

"Yes, I do. They scramble and fuzz your memories, so the dreams are not so vivid nor make much sense" She poured the milk, grabbed her cup, and sat back, reclined in the deep couch. "Some of them at least. Others were used for deep space travel. They kept the travellers from dreaming for years or decades even, so they would keep their minds intact when reaching the other side" She sipped her tea, put it back down, and sat back again. "They are also used for tracking. In the past they were used as a beacon from outer system missions. The foundation found out that by communicating through the mints, they could maintain a more stable connection and tracking. The mints were made obsolete after the last mission took off, a few centuries ago. Without missions, there was a large stock of unused consumables. However, they kept the manufacturing, mostly used now as pain-killers or antidepressants"

I argued "And you still gave them to me, to mess with my memories? Is that it?"

Carrie served a cup of coffee and handed it over to me. She nodded and waved the cup in front of my face. "No Dia, and you know that. The ones you had were special" she denied. "I imagine you remember what I told you about the mints. Those were modified versions, a formula less intense, but greatly more interesting. Someone managed to invert the composition of the mints and made them bring the memories close together. The memories then started working as magnets. The more the user dreamed, the stronger the binding force would be" I heard the clink of porcelain touch the wooden table. I was trying my best not to look in her eyes, because if I did, I didn't know if I would be able to feel if she was telling me everything. The other two I could only capture their position in the corners of my vision, one on each side.

"Homomorphic encryption" Adonis said quietly, but for everyone to hear. I played the record of those words through my mind. They sounded more real and meaningful coming out of his mouth then hearing it in my head. "Is that what it is?" he questioned.

Carrie tilted her head so she could meet his eyes, and lift her perfectly trimmed eyebrows "Hm, so you do know your lore" She leaned forward and changed her gaze, looking straight at me. "Dia, I have never done anything to harm you or to keep you from your objectives. I wanted you to find what happened to your mother as much as you did. But I just couldn't tell you, not directly" I finally gave in, and stared at her caramel eyes. "You had to find out by yourself"

"But why? Why couldn't you just tell me? Wouldn't it be so much easier?" I questioned.

"Chris, do you mind telling her?" I had almost forgot that he was there too, sitting in the same couch, in opposite ends. He denied looking at me too. We were too similar in many things, I thought.

"The scintillance was not an accident, at least not

in the way it was planned" Planned? I turned to face him, but he kept looking down on his feet. The scintillance was an accident. I know that. I remembered people talking about that, the news, the reconstruction, the foundation excuses. He continued "The scintillance was part of the foundation's space program. They were working on that since...very long" He looked up but aimed at Carrie. She nodded in agreement and let him finish. "A few months before it happened, I started to realise dad was acting strange. He loved his work, he always had, but for a while before he died, he only had eyes and ears for the project he was working on. He was coming home late, sometimes he would sleep in his office for a day or two, without letting anyone know. It was then that I decided to confront him about it. He wasn't angry or annoyed, barely blinking. He said he would take me to the office, because I needed to see what they were creating: a discovery of a lifetime, he said" He stopped suddenly and lower his head again.

"He wanted to show everyone the wonderful material the foundation managed to create. He thought it would be a good idea to try and use it to make something beautiful, useful even" Carrie picked up and carried on with the story.

"What did they create? What was this material?" I questioned.

"Damian and the engineering department were

working in a technology connected to the space program. They were working on a faster-than-light technology using gravitons as its main processor" I couldn't follow much but was paying attention. I glanced at Adonis, as he would be able to follow it all. "They have created the metal gravitonium. The foundation successfully conceived gravity in metal form" She paused and looked at Chris. "Damian died not a week after, before he could share his discovery with his son, due to radiation exposure"

No one spoke for what it felt like hours. Finally, Chris broke the silence. "I went after the foundation for answers, but they refused. They didn't even let me see him" I bit my lips. "And then I just couldn't stay here anymore"

"I'm sorry Chris" My mouth was dry, and my lips cut when I talked. "And what about my mom? And the scintillance?"

"I can answer both questions, but not entirely. Do you still want to hear it from me?" Carrie sarcastically asked.

"What do you mean not entirely? Even now, even after all you have hidden from me, you still want to keep me blind. For fuck sake, just say it" Perhaps I was losing my patience, perhaps I was actually believing her.

"Right. Answering you second question first. This

radioactive metal was going to be the fuel and source of their faster-than-light technology, testing it on their module, which they called the Precursor. The Precursor was sent to space a few centuries ago, in an attempt to use the last resources of an original foundation, before they disappeared, and had to be shut down. They have worked in the shadows, independently for all that time, until they were forgotten, a mere legend, so they could resurge as the corporation we know today" I could hear Chris impatiently and rhythmically count with his foot, a knock-knock that was both intensively annoying and oddly calming. He sighed loudly, stood up and walked to the window. I followed him with my gaze but switched to Carrie's when she resumed.

"At that time, gravitonium was not yet a reality, but they had hope in the future, it would be eventually discovered or created by someone. The original foundation then developed the prototype of what the mints are" She took a very familiar tin can from the inner pocket of her suit jacket and put it on the table. "They created these pills to help the crew's minds survive the journey. Even with the technology the foundation had in the past, they still could not get close to a fraction of the speed of light. They betted in the future" Carrie opened the can and took one of the small, white pucks, and held in front of her face "And, as a contingency plan, they inputted inside each of those mints, the seeds of their work. Each one of those pills have a part of the metal" I was perhaps more confused than before her story. I had so many questions, but none of those questions would make any sense. Maybe for Adonis, but not for me.

"And what does it mean?"

Carrie then uttered the words I have heard before, and that I have used too, as best as I could "Well Dia, that my dear, is the physical product of homomorphic encryption"

A quietness fell through the roof and squashed us three to the ground.

Carrie put the mint back in the tin. "These particles were divided, and their other halves are bound, naturally connected. They behave, move, and act as double, a pair. One moves, the other moves. When one dies, the other dies too. With that information, the foundation discovered that they could know anyone's location, given that the mints were consumed recently" She poured more tea in her cup, and sipped. "Cold, disgusting" Cup rested in the table, she continued. "But that doesn't explain the scintillance, does it?" A rhetorical question.

"Well, the crew of the Precursor took their mints, were tucked into their pods, and driven to unexplored, outer space. Such a marvellous adventure, right? But there were a couple things missing.

First, they needed to find where in the vast universe had the mission's journey ended. That was the easy part. As they planned, as soon as the crew woke up, they were given another dose of the mints. As soon as it was broken down on their stomachs, the signal resumed, and – success – they found them. A new system, a new beginning for humankind, a glorious new age" Carrie had a particular expertise for drama, and her pauses were building up to a middle of second act reveal. "However, and that now was the tricky part, they needed to bring them back, and after, be able to go back to that new, unexplored region. They decided to use the same homomorphic encryption that work so well with the dreams of memories. The two halves would behave and act in pairs. Therefore, if one of them were to be blown up, and implode into a black hole, the other, in the distant end of space, would also follow suit" She dropped that, and waited for someone to pick it up again.

"But, for them to collapse such a particle, they would have to brake it, right? But to destroy a particle that small, this destruction would have to be..." Adonis replied.

"Catastrophic" She said, ominously and dramatically as it should be.

A silence that has never been seen was playing loudly in the room. Chris was still looking outside from the window, Adonis looked down at his feet,

Carrie was looking at me, and I, well I was trying to make some sense of all that.

"So, they created the scintillance?" I mumbled to myself.

"Yes, and also no. You see, Damian was working on the project, and according to what he told us, they were very close to creating a controlled environment for their own scintillance. However..." And she looked to her left as Chris was coming back to the sofa. It felt almost planned, rehearsed between the two of them.

"Before he...dad calculated and worked out the outcome of this controlled blast, he noticed it would be much bigger than the accident we had six months ago" He breathed heavily and sat down in front of me now. "He went to his superiors, to try and show what would happen to the city and to the people if they went through with that. They shrugged off and dismissed what he found. They... they said that they were there for a reason"

I tried my best to look him in the eyes. We locked gaze, and for once I felt that my friend, my childhood friend, was there again.

"So what did he do?" I asked.

Chris said quietly "Gravitonium is hard to come by. It takes a lot of energy and not much was made. It took them years to make just a small piece. At the time, they had a little lingot, that would be used to bring the Precursor back. He wanted to take it, to steal it, bring it as far as possible from the foundation. Him and your mother were planning a heist. To steal the metal, and take it away, as far as they could, and then hide it. But…" His stare lowered, his hands held the back of his neck. I couldn't do anything then, and because of that I forced myself to touch his knee.

"So, why did the scintillance still happened?" I questioned, as I believed that there were parts of that story that I wasn't been told, not yet.

"Damian couldn't stop it, and he was gone before they could act on their plan" Carrie then continued. "If it weren't for him, maybe we wouldn't be here now. But your mother, she kept going and decided that she would put the plan in action. And she did. However, due to gravitonium's high volatility, as soon as it was taken from its containment…" with those words uttered, she stood up, open her tin can, and swallowed one of the mints.

"Okay, and what about my mother" I reminded her.

"Yes, your mother" she turned around and handed me an old, yellowed envelop, with a couple colourful stickers, and my name written on it. "I cannot tell you that, Dia"

I jolted up and was ready to destroy her with all the

horrible things I had been concocting in my mind for a moment like this. But before I could even open my mouth, she kept talking.

"I know that was not what you wanted to hear, but that is the truth. I cannot tell you because I don't know entirely what happened myself. This envelope was never opened since the day she was gone. She handed it to me and told me to give it to you when the moment was right. I didn't know when that moment was, until now. I believe you will find what you need to know in there. I am sorry not been able to help you more, and to have put you in this position." Carrie was determined, direct, caring, but at that moment, that last sentence sounded tired, defeated even.

"What position? What is happening Carrie?" I was many levels of confused. She didn't answer. She looked at her watch, unfastened it from her wrist, and held it to the light.

"I wanted to show you more about watches too. I wanted to be able to show you more, like this one. This is my favourite" She then proceeded to wind the wristwatch "The crunch of the gears is so satisfying. Listen. The sound of time itself chewing" She smiled, sighed, and with that last sigh she pushed the smile out of her face. She turned and looked at where Chris and I were seated. "Chris, I'm sorry too. I ended up putting you in danger as well" He turned to where she was, only a shape against the light coming through the window. He also seemed confused, intrigued. She walked towards Adonis, crouched down, and they both stared at each other. She handed him the tin of mints, and closed his hand around it, holding it tight with both hands.

"What you're talking about?" He asked on my behalf. "Why are you saying that now? That's nothing to do with what we have to do"

"But it is" She got closer to the window again and touch the glass with her forehead. Just staring down at something only she could possibly know. "Dia, you will find your mother. I hope that you find all you need to know on that envelope, and possibly even more" without even moving, she cleaned her throat and continued "And Chris, you have to go with her now. I believe that you will also find what you are looking for, if you stick together with your friends" Carrie turned around, leaning back against the window, looking at us. "Dia, you have to go with Adonis. He knows more than he understands, and because of that, he is in as much danger as you are now. He will help you find your memories" A faded smiled twisted the corner of her lips, as she cleaned the thin red line coming down her nose.

"Carrie" I asked and gasped and called for her. "What you're saying? Why can't you come with us? You need to. You need to help us. You have to help me" I sobbed those last words. I tried to go to where she was, maybe I could just drag her. She needed to come and help, she owned that.

But I was held by Chris. He didn't even need to put force, he just touched my arm, and I paused, and looked at his face. His eyes were locked onto Carrie's. Big, black, drowning eyes, piercing the whole distance between the two.

"Chris" I said his name, and that felt terminal. "Why?"

"We have to go Dia" The sound came out of his mouth, but it didn't sound like him. It was another person, much wiser, older, jaded. "Now!"

"But, what about Carrie?" I questioned, and I thought I fought, but I didn't. I wish I had.

"They're coming Dia. We cannot stay" Adonis said from the other side, waking up from his own daydreaming. Chris let me go, grabbed his pack, and walked towards the door. I watched the whole thing in a fast forward slow-motion, a timeless unfolding of events.

"They don't know that we're here" I said that as if I knew who they were, as if I knew what the fuck was going on. "We can go together, the four of us. Carrie?"

"They are coming now Dia. Coming for me. They know. I told them. Just go now" Carrie was clenching at the window parapet; I could see her hand twitching and her knuckles white, and her shoulders trembling. She coughed twice. From the other side of the room, I couldn't clearly discern between her crimson lipstick and the blood in the corner of her mouth.

"Dia" I heard a voice, muffled through all the sounds and voices and memories going through my mind then. I wished then that I were still just a little girl, watching my mom working at her office, without any concerns, without any desires, no imminent disaster, no foundation, no lies, nothing. I wished to be back there, to even hear the clang of the hammer to the metal, the hushed whisper of the water colling the heated blade, smell of smoke and dust and fire. Too many sounds. And then I was pulled from all that, jerked out of that peaceful wishful thinking.

"Dia, we have to go. Now!" I looked at his eyes. Maybe desperation, maybe conviction, maybe just fear and confusion, as mine would also have shown. "Carrie" Adonis said, after moving back to the door, and pulling me along.

"They're here already. Just go!" And with that, we were gone.

The next few moments were blurred, fast, and instinctive. There were stairs, a door, people talking, the back door, and then fresh air, light, and we were walking fast away from the flat, and from Carrie. For the last time.

The ground floor was packed with cars and people. Some of those were wearing white helmets and body armours and were holding weapons. We haven't seen weapons in the daylight. I have never seen the enforcers that close. The closest thing I remembered was seeing them during one of the foundation's announcements, but never in the flesh. We continued through the back exit, moving quietly but fast. The back gate was so close, almost at arm's length. I managed to jump it quite quickly, and then Chris followed, awkwardly, with Adonis helping him on the other side. We were almost gone.

"Hey, you there" and then we heard someone shouting. A static noise and a beep, and the voice grew bigger, enveloping the whole building. "Stop where you are sir. This is an enforced restricted area. Please stop until you are promptly verified"

"Come Adonis, come quick. What the fuck are you waiting?" I tried to open the gate somehow, but it was shut, and was not budging. "Chris, help me here. Help me pull the gate, come on"

"You have to go Dia. You both, just go" He turned around, showed his back to the two of us on the other side of the gate.

"What!? No, no you can't. Shit, you have to come

already, they're almost here Adonis" I turned to Chris "Tell him Chris, tell him that he needs to come quick"

He stood still "He's right Dia, we have to go"

"Are you fucking insane?" I grabbed him by his shirt collar.

"Dia" Adonis said, without looking at me. "Just go already. They have only seen me; they think I'm alone. I can think of something to ahn...I don't know, I'll figure it out" His hands were closing and opening back again. "It's going to be fine"

I couldn't believe what was happening. I was paralysed. I couldn't move. I just heard Chris saying, "Come on, let's go" and I felt myself being pulled from somewhere, taken somewhere else.

***

Chris and I walked for almost an hour, hiding our faces, looking behind our shoulders, peeping through corners and alleys. I could smell the river again. The rain made the mud and the dirt so fragrant, and the grass, and herbs and small insects so much more alive and mobile. We stood there, by the large trees in the riverbank for a few minutes, catching our breath and collecting our senses. There wasn't much I wanted to collect, however. The whole way there, I was thinking about Adonis'. I wanted to go back, to be there with him, to take him back with us. I had to find him.

And then Carrie's speech. Again, fooled and be-trayed by her. Again, kept from a knowledge that could've helped me in my search. Again, helplessly driven away by her. I wanted to be angry, I wanted to hate her, and to despise her, and to break the memories I had from her. I wanted to tell her all that. I wanted to tell her how she had ruined our friendship, how she has been nothing more than dishonest with me, how she had known things about myself that not even I could remember. My heart was filled with rage and anger, and my tongue was on fire, ready to burn the very memory of her. But I couldn't.

She was still Carrie, the one who cared for me when I had nothing, the one who tried to protect me, in her own way, through her own trials, by her own mistakes, until the end. I held that anger, and swallowed that fire, and that burned, burned so much, so deep, it could melt metal, it could forge a blade so sharp. And I kept that blade, and sheathed it, and held it close to my heart.

We haven't spoken for some time. I didn't know how long. I was gripping my hands so hard, that it wasn't until then that I let go. The muscles in my arms were aching, and my shoulder were stiff. My left hand still held her watch.

I just remember saying "It's getting dark. We

should go home" I stood up, wrapped the watch around my wrist. The cold metal was a balm to my burning arms. "Come one" Chris was still on the ground, contemplating what we had been through. I held my hand in front of him and called him up. "Let's go"

He pulled himself up, cleaned his trousers, and without saying a word, he held me in his arms. I had no idea how to mourn. I could even mourn my mother, or to save Adonis, and now Carrie. I was trying to keep my anger inside, and by doing that I let something else out. My arms wrapped around Chris' chest, and I cried.

***

ON ACCEPTANCE

I was staring at the ceiling for an hour since I have woken up. The gentle light coming from the edges of the closed door, the sound of people talking, the smooth and familiar bed. I have waited for Mal to ask us everything, for Chris to get comfortable, and for myself to digest, and then vomit it out, what happened then. Carrie was gone, I was handed a letter from my mother kept from me, the three of us were being chased by the foundation, and they had Adonis with them. I read the letter three times, the three times it felt different, one sad, one proud, and one afraid.

I tried to read in my mom's voice, but I couldn't remember it, I just couldn't hear her speak, not in my memory and not in my dreams. I choose Carrie's voice instead.

And she spoke of many things, of things of the past, things of now, and things that will come to be one day. Also, she talked of things that I will never speak out loud, things that are only for me, things only I can hear and understand.

But of the things pertinent to what was happening, she had this to say.

"Dia, my pretty daylight, I wish we could have stayed together. As you are reading this, I am not there to say those words to you. But you know that everything I write down, everything you read is the truth, under the sun truth.

I am writing and rushing now, because what we made, what we discovered, is something so precious, and so incredible, but also very dangerous. We don't know how dangerous, not even what it can do entirely.

Damian and I, we spent a long time looking and trying to find the reasons and motives behind the Precursor. People don't know that name, and those who do hear it as a mythical name, a fable, a prophet's tale.

This name was lost in the past, before our time in this world, before everyone's time. But the Precursor is the reason for all that we are doing here my love. ARIA, the foundation, the city, the county, the technology, and the research, is all because of it.

You know all that because I have told you. It is hidden, secret and protected inside your head. At this moment, you need to know about you, and why you don't know, and what we have made.

Dia, we have made it possible for gravity to be forged and folded and turned into metal. As soon as we have successfully created a nugget, we have been brought into the core of ARIA. We have been summoned. We were told about the Precursor, the quest for the unsurmountable universal traverse, and the scintillance.

First of all, the scintillance was not an accident. What happened was a demonstration of what we have made. We had to stop the foundation and for that, we have decided to use the nugget of gravitonium. We will kill their project, because what they would have caused with planning, would be infinitely larger than the spark we will make today.

Second, you have triggered the scintillance. I don't know if you remember me as you read this letter, but that is the truth. Under the sun truth. We found that the exposure to the metal's unusual radioactivity affects long term memory. And you, more than anyone else, have been in contact with it the most. Too much in fact. Intimately and deadly. You have melted, folded, and forged the metal into a blade. A blade of blue that have cut you profoundly. You have survived, and that was a miracle. We haven't.

Thirdly, I am not gone. I am lost, I was lost, but as I write this, I am still next to you. If the blade almost killed you, it took me away, far away, but I somehow can see myself. I see myself writing this letter, I see myself, and Damian, fading away as the blade itself cuts the very air inside the lab, and I can see me looking at myself. I don't understand it, not yet, maybe not ever, but I know that what I see is the truth.

As I write this, we are rushing, and we are dying, but we have all the time in the world. I have you next to me, and I see you now.

Dia, my pretty daylight, go and remember me"

I held that letter hard, crumpled the paper in my hands, and didn't let it go. I now knew all of that, but I still didn't remember anything. I made the blade, not my mom; I triggered the scintillance, not her; I stopped the foundation once; we both.

The fourth time I read the letter, the sun was already shining outside, the morning mist from the river was now surrounding us. And that was the last time I read my mother's letter. I have been told things, things I did, things I made, things I were, but after all that, I still couldn't see myself being all that. Not yet at least.

I wouldn't be sleeping anymore. Not after that, and not before what I was going to be doing. I rubbed my eyes, saw the spiralling lights and colours, and let my vision simmer in the slow light of the young day. I let myself drown in that view for a minute. I thought of the way my mother wrote, and I liked to believe I had internal monologues similar to those words. Sometimes vague, sometimes profound, most of the times over dramatic.

With one single movement I pulled myself up from the bed and stood up, stretching and moaning softly. Tied my hair up, pulled up my trousers, and touched the scar in my chest with my shirt unbuttoned. It never actually hurt, I thought as I felt it with the tip of my fingers. It doesn't hurt now, as if it was always there there, as if it had never been open before.

In the living room, Chris was still sleeping in the couch. He looked tired. Tired of many things I suppose. Of lying to me, of running away, of leaving things behind. As I was looking to find my own story, he also had grudges and debts to be paid. His father, his own part on this whole story. I found myself seating down at the edge of the couch.

"We have to go" I said quietly, not for him "We have to find out what happened. I have to look at my memories, and then" I didn't know what else to say "Then I might find out what to do"

He didn't reply. He barely moved in his sleep. He was tired. It was good that he was sleeping. He needed rest, and I needed to find out who I was and what I had done. I needed to look at my memories.

I washed my face, put my shoes, grabbed a yesterday's croissant in the living room bowl, and was ready to go out.

"Dia, are you going already?" Mal said from the sliver that was her room's door half open. She made sure to keep quiet.

"Yeah. I'm sorry Mal, I cannot tell you know, but

I promise I will" I said in between bites "At this point, you know enough, or maybe too much even, I'm not sure. But I have to go now, and alone" I looked back at the couch. "He will understand. Just tell him I went to the office, and will be back"

"Alright" Mal said, restrained in her words as I've never seen.

"It'll be okay. See you later" I said that half believing.

Leaving Chris behind was either the best idea or the worst. I didn't know if it would be dangerous, I didn't know if he would make me not go, I still didn't trust him, not fully. I decided that this was a choice I had to make myself. No one pushing me to one side, or pulling me to another, no lies. I was looking for the truth, under the sun truth.

***

There was just one place to go now. I had to look at my memories and finally put the pieces together, and I needed Adonis to help me do it.

He let me know, in the dead of night, that I should meet him at the office. I brought my pad up and sent Adonis a message. His business card was remarkably simple, but it had an elegance that only precision and coordination could give. His full name on one side, "Adonis Manuel" and on the other, his title "chief engineer" and his pad call number.

"Hi. I'm coming over. I want to help", I wrote and sent it, more like a decision than a request I noticed. I barely knew him. But I felt, deep inside, that I should trust him, and his sister. But they seemed to be desperate enough to have brought me in, showed me their toys, and asked me to come and play together. I had no interest in helping their project in any way, but the hope to look at the dreams, to actually look and find real information, that I couldn't stop thinking about.

I walked for almost an hour, under the cover of the mist and the trees, I could already see the foundation's buildings, the small rapids forming in the river because of the crater, and the crate itself. The mist surrounded the perimeter of the crater from its base all the way to the skies, circling and rotating around it as a pilar, impenetrable, invisible, and still there.

As I came out from behind the treeline and moved to the main road, the noise was getting louder and louder. People moving, mostly in groups, talking loudly, scared almost. Rushing past the green in front of the main building, both employees and visitors alike. Maybe a fire alarm had been set off, and everyone needed to be walked off the site. Odd, for there was no ringing sound, no siren, no firepro staff orienting and coordinating the exit of people. There was a quiet panic, too silent and eerie.

And there they were. The town has not seen fire weapons for so long, that even having looked directly at a group of enforcers just the day before, it still felt off, seen them casually strolling around, or in this case, herding people out of the foundation's complex. No one had seen them since the foundation stablished itself in the area perhaps. Their investment in infrastructure, education, and research affected the overall security and policing too. I don't remember any of that, I was maybe too small, but it was when we moved to the new house that mom noticed. She used to say "it's strange that I have to ask you to come home earlier now. but please still do Dia, there's always something out there". I thought she was just overprotective, or that our life earlier, in the outskirts, was just plainly more dangerous, but maybe she was right. Maybe there was always something out there, something we couldn't see.

I watched the enforcers bring people out of the building by the dozens, hidden behind the trees that opened up to the walking path that followed the river and surrounded the facility. Maybe that was for me? Maybe what I had been put into was more than I thought, more than I understood. I didn't move, tried to be as quiet and as immobile as possible. I needed to keep watching, however.

My pad buzzed and vibrated, and I muffled a shout, dropping to the ground trying to find the damn gadget, and run back behind the tree. I sat with my back against the thick trunk, looked up to-wards the canopy, pulling and pushing air as deep and as fast as I could. I was scared, intuitively and instinctively my body jerked to hide from them. Thoughts and ideas ran through my mind.

The noise continued, far and distant, no change in its patterns, not getting louder, no shouting or steps toward me. I took a last deep breath. The cold mist still smelling of dirt and dew and damp. I turned to look to be sure I was not being chased, and to be sure I could finally check my pad. All was still the same. I saw the silhouettes moving in the distance, already freed from the shrouding of the morning fog. I took another breath, this a calmer, resolute one, a decisive air took over my lungs.

I turned back and sat again protected by the tree. Took the pad out of my back pocket, and the cracked screen was showing a single icon, a tri-angle with an arrow moving from left to right. I selected it and the message popped up. It said, in a single line, in a single breath "don't come! Stay away!". I stared at the text for a minute, wishing I hadn't come all this way, wishing I didn't find what I had found just a day earlier. Because if I hadn't known all that, I might have listened to the warning.

***

I found myself sneaking behind the foundation's

buildings. The enforcers were mainly focused on the people inside or in the front of the building, and they're trying to take people outside. Probably they weren't that keen on keeping anyone from coming in. At least not from the muddy, slopy riverbank, snaking behind the back gardens, between the crater and the back of the minor, less imposing buildings. Except for the majestic ARIA headquarters, the buildings surroundings were not as interesting, nor impressive. They were very functional, streamlined, dark-blue concrete blocks attached to the principal area. While the ARIA HQ was beautiful in a very digestive and obvious way, the smaller, utilitarian workstations had no beauty, no attraction whatsoever. They were the fungal growth living a symbiotic life under the glorious orchid.

The mud and dampness crawled all the way to my knees. It was somehow cold and warm at the same time, every step I took into the wet ground. After a few minutes, always monitoring the sounds coming from the other side of the constructions, I managed to reach the backside of the old church. Compared with the rest of the foundation, the old church felt more like a dead ingrown nail, stuck and falling apart. There were no one here, but I could still hear the enforcers shouting and directing the others outside. Maybe there were no one in the office at that time. I wasn't and I knew that Mal was at home. Perhaps they had already surveyed this area and had moved to the other buildings. Maybe they were still coming this way. There was no way to know for sure, so I quickly moved towards the back door. It was the only door that still used a mechanical cylinder lock, and I was the only one that had used that door since, well ever. The door led to the dressing rooms of the now imploded pool, and the toilet. The back entrance had been forgotten and underused, which turned out extremely fortunate to me in that moment. I picked the lock, as I would normally do, got it, and closed the door behind me. It was Chris who taught me how to lockpick, or at least that was what my memories were telling me.

Even though I have made myself believe that there was no one surveying the old church, it would not be of bad behaviour to keep it as quiet as possible. And as soon as I pushed the door softly and heard the faint click of the lock, I noticed the voices coming from the office.

"Fuck" I shouted, in my most silent inner voice to myself. They were there already, and for the sound of it, they were looking for something, or someone, but at that point I knew they were looking for me. Something in my instinct, my memories, or my dreams triggered a safety alarm in my head, and in my heart, I knew that all of that agitation was because of me.

As I got closer, creeping towards the opening leading to the main hall, the voices started to sound less like noise and more like almost intelligible mumble. They sounded agitated and hasty, but much less commanding and official than the enforcers on the other side. A woman's voice, flat and determined, but almost raspy, and a man's, less sure of itself, fumbling with the sounds it was trying to create. From where I was, and by pressing my face against the doorframe, I could see the glass door leading to the other buildings, and to the engineering wing, the first cubicle and half of my desk and all my stuff – so much stuff – and the shadows of the voice holders, faintly cast and stretched through the floor and at the wall behind them. The colours of the sunlight hitting the stained-glass windows were a kaleidoscope of reflections, drawing patterns in the whole office where the fading shadows frantically gesticulate and moved.

After a few seconds appreciating the light and shadows puppet show, I realised I knew the owner of those voices. I was there because of them. They were the whole reason I walked and hide and stuffed my leg in the mud not to be caught. There were no other voices in the room, that I was sure, which gave me the security to assume they were not there there along with the enforcers and maybe, just maybe, were there because of the message I sent on my way. I wanted to take a risk, and I did.

"Adonis" I said accomplished, walking out of the bathroom. "Is that you?" I questioned him in particular, because I messaged him, and because his sister still frightened me.

Adonis looked at me through his sister, his face paralysed, his mouth open, his jaw hanging by his knees, while Vóra, who had her back against me, turned quickly one her good leg, her eyes sharp and so dark. He walked slowly but firmly towards me, and when he got close, too close, he held me in an awkward hug. "You're okay?" I asked, and hugged him back.

Vóra sprinted in our direction, her limp quite visible now, caught her by surprise, she readjusted her pace, and reached us. She held my arm, broke us two, her face so close to mine then, and raised a finger across her pierced, angry lips.

"Shut up" Vóra chased me, in a shushed hiss. "What are you doing here? Didn't you see what is going outside? Didn't you read the text I sent you. Shit!" she then let go of my arm, but I could still feel the outlined of the thin fingers gripping my skin. She swung her head and called her brother to come to where they were, which he did unquestionably.

"Dia, what…why did you come?" Adonis asked me quietly and gently, but still uneasy.

"I come because you wanted me to. You wanted

me to help you, to find out about the dreams, and the memories. The scintillance" I said as sure as I could. "I know I should've come earlier, but I had a few things to do before, and when I see your message Adonis…"

"We haven't asked you to come" Vóra hissed at me again. "Did you get a pad message from him?" She pointed to her brother. I nodded affirmatively, and she snapped. "Fuck, so they're interfering with the pads now. And you replied?" I nodded again. "Great. That's perfect. You could have kept your mouth shut, you could've done so much" And she looked at her brother again. "But now, we have to clean up your mess, again" So quiet, so sibilant, and so enraged.

"Wait, what are you saying?" I didn't believe I had done that much damage.

"You know how much trouble we had to go through to explain what he was doing at your friend's apartment block? Do you? I bet not. And now we have to clean up your mess, again" Vóra finished, breathing heavily, her hands on her hips.

Adonis touched his sister's arm and, looking at me, said "She doesn't know yet. And whatever she had done to help me, that would have triggered this whole situation anyway, or even a worse one" No hiccupping on words. "We have to move Dia. Vóra and I were looking for you since yesterday, but as soon as the enforcers started to herd people out of the building, we decided that we had to erase you first, as much as we could, before we could act again" Erase me. That stabbed me so intensely, in my guts, such violation.

"What are you both talking about? What have I done? I haven't done anything" I forgot to go quietly for a second and shouted at them both. I wanted to run, wanted to go back home, lie in bed and wait for everything to pass.

But as I said that, heavy knocks sounded on the door. Three in sequence, rushed, brute. "Open up! Open this door now!" The enforcing, a word and a being I have only known as a tale, fantasy that the foundation told the town, as their security and safety policies. "We will keep you all safe, and will enforce the peace we all deserve", they said. And then, the same peace was knocking at the door, brute.

Three knocks again, and the same speech. Adonis and Vóra looked at each other, and then at me. She jolted towards the door and was handling open live wires in the panel next to it. "We cannot use the pads here. They are tracking us. Do you have yours with you?" He asked as his sister was touching wires together and picking an electronic lock. "Yes", I said. "Ow!" A big spark and the doors moved a little, creating an opening, that Vóra managed to hold it open. "Come on! It will restart in a minute. Just leave the pad there and come" We were looking at her holding that door by herself while the flickering panel sparkled.

I took my pad and dropped it by me feet. "Alright" I managed to say "Let's go. And then you both will fucking tell me what's going on" I pulled Adonis by the arm. I took one side of the door and held it, while Vóra positioned herself on the other side. Adonis went through, then me, then his sister. The door closed, and all the light, all the colour, and all the sounds were gone, jailed behind the thick, prismatic glass. Behind us, the long, dark, flickering corridor. The maze of hallways and sombre lights was even more disturbing in the dark.

***

ON FINDINGS

We have twenty minutes now, after that I don't know how much more the door will hold" Vóra urgently announced that from the other side of the lab. They have set up the machine and have prepared it for me to be connected to it. As Adonis mentioned on our way there, "We call the machine Postverta. It captures electromagnetic waves that are generated in dreams. These waves, theta waves, are then captured and stored in our hardware, and then categorized. After they are structured based on their intensity and resolution, they are sent through an algorithm that addresses the subjective content of those dreams, compiling them into multiple timelines, an uncountable number of possible outcomes and journeys that those memories could have been through. The algorithm is called Anteverta", of which I was intensively trying to hold on to their names. Postverta and Anteverta. "Almost there" Adonis replied. "Ante is taking its time loading the algorithm. It ahn...shouldn't take too long" He turned to me and asked "Are you okay? Ready?" I didn't know what to say at that point, on that state, linked to a machine that would pigeonhole my dreams and vomit it out, in a beautiful, precise, inorganic train of thought.

"Yes, I should be. We're here now" I told myself that more than answered his question. I was scared. Not at the machine, not at the wires attached to my forehead, not at the people trying to get in, not even at the risks that an experience such as that could provide. I was terrified to finally know the whole truth. To see myself, the Dia on the ceiling, and look down at myself, knowing, judging, and maybe frustrating. "Just don't fry my brain, okay? I need it to remember to kick your ass if that doesn't tell me anything" Jokes normally made things easier, less serious, less fulfilled. Now it just reminded me of Carrie, and Chris, and my mother. I would see them all again now.

"Right, screw the chattering you two. Are we ready? Can you turn it on already?" Vóra was not only aggressively trying to make this work, but she was also scared. Scared of the ones she was keeping outside, maybe of something else, maybe simply scared of the whole transformation that everything would go through as soon as my memories were brought back to me.

"Yes, yes, that's ready now. Ante is on, Post is loading the program now. How much longer Vóra?" Adonis shouted over the now very loud electronic hum from the machine.

"Seventeen minutes. Shit. They're brute forcing the entrance. Shit, shit. That's not good Donis. Still loading?" Vóra shouted back.

"Still loading. Maybe ahn...two more minutes at least for the whole algorithm to be transferred, and then I just need to set it up and we're good to go" He said whilst trying to rush the impious computer.

"Can I do anything?" I suggested in the midst of chaos.

"Yes!" Vóra turned and spoke. "Pay attention to everything. Everything is important. We are collecting the data, but the actual information is on you to decipher" She turned back to her screen abruptly "Shit. Donis, they breached the main entrance. They're five minutes earlier than I was expecting. Is it done? Please say it's done"

"All done. Yes, all done. Great ahn..." He fumbled and moved towards me, grabbed my hand, and with his other gave me a couple of mints. "Take them, they'll ahn...make you dream easier" I took them and swallow.

And nothing happened. It was all the same. All the same. Until everything stopped. I saw Vóra shouting at the screen, paralysed. I turned to Adonis, who was also frozen, unmoving. I started noticing that the air was also stuck on itself, not a breeze, not a breath, not a breath in nor a breath out.

"What is different about those mints? Did you do anything with them?" I asked as I swallowed the pills and closed my eyes.

***

And when you're walking through a corridor and if feels you been walking there forever or just for a few seconds, and all the doors are the same, and the pillars are the same, copies of each other, and there is no end nor beginning, is just a corridor that you walk through, and you don't know how actually you ended up in that corridor. How did you arrive there? Why are you there? Where are you going? And you have the feeling that you are being watched or followed or that your actions have already been decided and everything is premeditated. Then a worry, a crunching concern starts flaring up in your heart, and in your stomach, and in the back of your head, and it builds up, through the shivers up your nerves. That worry is so serious and so catastrophically crucial, that the outcome of the day depends on it, and maybe even your own life, and the whole world's existence too, why not? Why haven't you done it? You've done it wrong. You should've made it different, or the same. Why have you done it? The worries crawl in pulses right behind your ears, and up your throat, and up the inside of your thighs, pushing your sternum, making it scratch. The knot on your mouth is so intense now, your life depends on that worry, on the concern that you haven't made it.

But that is it. A concern, just a concern. Have you ever felt it? Are you feeling it now?

"Yes" I thought I responded, but I wasn't sure I had

even moved my mouth at all.

Good. That is fine, that is good. You are not in the corridor anymore, you see? You do not have to worry about that. You are fine. Under the water is safe. See? You can breathe and you are already swimming. What are you seeing? Look up. All the lights rushing past you now. So pretty, no? Look at that one there. The blue one. Look how it is trying to push back and swim against the flow of the river. It is too small unfortunately. Oh, so small, so fragile, but it keeps trying. Look! Swirling around the feet. Such strength in such small container, right? But the river, oh the river is no ally to those who fight against it. It tears them apart, it pulls, and it crushes, and it shreds it to pieces. That blue, it is fighting for its life. Do you think its running through a corridor too? Do you think it has worries too? Don't answer, just look at it. Oh, my dear, just let go, let go, it's okay. Go with all the other colours. There it goes. Where are you now?

"I'm here" *I tried to move my mouth, but nothing was moving.*

Yes, yes you are. You're here now. Look. You're there, you see? Below. Look down there.

"It's...me" *I looked down and saw myself seating at the chair at Carrie's flat.* "I'm there"

Yes, you are. Good, you are. You are so peaceful, so sleepy. You are dreaming now. Look, you are desperately trying to catch those memories, but they are so flimsy, so plumy, far away, stuck in the ceiling. But that doesn't matter now. Close your eyes and open them again. Where we are now?

I was not in the living room anymore. I saw myself lying in my bed, loose, weak and broken, mouth ajar, drooling, sleeping the sleep of tiredness, stress, and the first taste of mints. "I see me"

Yes, oh yes, it is you. Do you see? You are dreaming now, you are dreaming of this now, of you, of memories. Oh, poor child, look at her, so small, so young, so innocent of what has happened. You were running away for so long, and you ended up there, was that what they told you?

"Yes" *I replied, aware that my muscles were not under my control.*

Yes, poor child. No, you were not running away. You see, you were running towards. Different directions, same magnitude. Those memories are so broken now my dear, so disperse, flung across the whole universe when you made it. Do you want to see it perhaps? Would that make you happy?

"Yes" *Again, I murmured without moving.*

Oh yes, good. Now, do it again. Close your eyes and open them again, wide now. Do you see? Do you know where we are now?

"ARIA" *I could only muster that.*

ARIA, yes. A name that this is called now, a name that is so new, so young, so inconsequent. You are here, see? Look! It is you, and your mother, and your friends, right? All of them, all together. What are their names? Do you remember?

"Adonis...Vóra...mom" I told.

Yes, correct. They are all there. And look. Hammer, thongs, anvil, fire and water. What are you about to do? It is so bright, every time you hammer down you make light. Oh, so beautiful. The blue and the silver merging, and folding, and burning, and being smashed between your hammer and the anvil.

Do you dream of that? Have you ever dreamed of what is happening now? No, right? Oh, that's exciting. You are taking that for yourself. Yes, you are. Don't protest now, look. You desire that power too, you all, but mostly her. They have asked you to make the blade. And look, they not happy with that. Do you see? They are trying to stop you, it sounds like. Can you hear? Oh, that's fine. I will tell you, do not worry.

You are hitting the blade, and the rest are discussing. Such misunderstanding, oh dear. Oh, and can you hear? More people coming to where we are. So many steps, and boots, and violence, so much violence.

And you keep making sparks, long, bright, deadly sparks. The boy is blind now, oh no. they run, you protest again, one stay behind. The footsteps, so close, so close. Shall we move on?

"No…I need…to see…" My voice was nothing there, silence in a silent world.

No, my dear, that story is over. You see, this is your story, not hers, and we have to follow you. Hurry now, let's catch up. Look now, they are going back. For what? For more? The metal pulls them all, it embraces them all, and terrorizes them all. An urge to hold it, to look at it, to be it, to be in it. And pulls, strongly, constantly. It pulls everything, it pulls everyone, like a whirlpool that engulfs the lost ship, a cylinder of death and suffering, and hope. Turning and twisting, feeding a possibility of life, of escape. No, not now, not for them. They belong to it now.

But look, it is you that matter, my dear. Only you. Do you remember that?

"No…yes"

Oh, that is a missing block. You are holding the blade, aren't you? Such beauty, such deadly beauty. What do you feel now? What does a memory feel after all? Is it a way to protect yourself from what you did? That's why you forgot? Look, did you see? How many people you hurt? Because of you, because of your memories, they are no longer here. They are gone, gone, gone!

"No…" the air pushed hardly through my tongue and my lips.

No? Oh dear, as if you controlled any of this. Do you see it now? How quaint. How franticly amused you *look now. In the deepest shadows of your brain, in the grossest recollection of your guts and inner organs, in the most unclean crevasses of the whirls and wrinkles of your being, you are but meat and bone, blood and time that passes through it, passes so thoroughly, so soundly. That is all you are, shameless fear and innocence, creating, making, machining, forging silly toys to try and fool time, to try and make it forget you, make it go away. No, my dear, you can't make it go, you feel the threads and the tracks of time through your leather and through your hairs. It becomes hard and dry and grey, and then it becomes dust, and then it becomes food.*

Come on. Wake up, we are almost done. Look, it is you and the other one. And that is your house. That is the only things that exists now. That is the only things that matters now. You are making all this happen. And you can't remember? Weak flesh. But now, oh, that is interesting. A sacrifice, your sacrifice. Brave girl. And you are taking that, edged heart, ember hearth. The blue gleam is gone. Did you see? Is gone now.

"Yes, it is" my eyes were closed, and I could see it all.

Now you know. Memories are so vain, they believe they know how to tell stories, but they are simply scattered pictures, thrown in the wind, in the hope that they will fall back in order by ordinance. No, memories don't tell stories, they are but patchwork, but cracked sky, vain and proud of a tale they haven't written. Do you remember now? Do you see what you needed to see?

"Yes" strangely the strength came back to my voice, even though my lips did not move.

Good, that's good my dear. Shall we go back then, I am now tired of telling stories, because I don't tell stories. I get tired. I am very tired now, and you should go.

***

Everything was blurred. I rubbed my eyes, and the familiar flair of stars and colours populated my view, until the office and the books and the machines came back into view.

"We ahn...have altered their composition, made them stronger in some ways, weaker in others, and less prone for tracing too" Adonis said, muffled at the start, and gradually his voice was opening, opening, until my ears captured the full sound. Everything looked and sounded strangely off putting, as if I had been there, in that same place, but hours before.

"What are you talking about? My mouth is so dry, feel like I can vomit" hangover, I tried to move, but I was still connected to the machine. A shrill of panic rushed up my spine. "How long have I been out? Are they in already?" I shouted, trying to free myself from the chair.

"What? No, you have to sleep and dream, idiot!

Fuck, can't you do anything right?" Vóra yelled from the other side, while typing frenetically. "You've been sitting there doing nothing for two minutes and now you want to go?" She shrugged "Shit, ten minutes Donis! How are we doing with that?"

Silence for a second. Vóra turned around to look at her brother. I was simply a passive existence at that moment.

"Donis! Wake up! Is she ready or not?" her voice was harsh, breaking a little, but when she talked with him, even swearing felt like caring.

"It's done" He finally said, coming out of the trance. "It's done Vóra"

"Great" she replied, "Can we start then?"

"No" Adonis murmured. Both myself and his sister turned and questioned at the same time. He was smiling now. "It's done. She went and came back. We did it Vóra"

"We did?" Vóra stopped typing, stopped blinking, stopped breathing. And then, as a statue that is brought back to life, she sprinted down the stairs, with a beam on her face, a face which I have never seen not frownng. Genuine happiness. The siblings giggling, hugging each other, spinning and spinning. "We did it" She said a last time. "We have to go now"

The two came towards me and proceeded to free my hands and my head from the machine. "Did you see anything? Do you remember anything?" her voice was much more curious now, different from the aggressive tone of earlier.

"Yeah, I think so. How long have I've been sleeping?" I felt as I spent hours in that dream. Hours, seeing my mother, Chris. They were there too. "I saw you. You both. I was taken and shown things. Events. Memories she said. But I don't remember having those memories. I know they were mine, and I feel that they are real, but I have no recollection of living through them"

"You have been ahn...asleep...for about two minutes maybe. It was so fast" Adonis finished untying my waist from the back of the chair, while his sister was working on my hands. "You said..."

She didn't let him finish "Did you see what happened? When you saw us? Did it show it to you?" She kneeled in front of me and looked me in the eyes. "Did you see his eyes? Did you see what you did to him?" Pointing at her brother, Vóra was starting, gnarling with her eyes.

Was all that real? Did that actually happen?

"Yes. I did" I turned to him "I'm sorry, I didn't mean to"

"No, you didn't, but it happened anyway. He

could've died, the both of us could. Shit, we held that lab for you to make whatever you had to make, a fucking knife, and then scram. And you left us there. Me, him, your own mother" More impatient than angry, she told me what I had seen earlier. "We managed to get away before the whole thing went off. It was your mother who came back and held the reaction. We didn't want to go, we wanted to help her, but she said"

"She said that we needed to find you" Adonis finished her sentence. "I saw that later, in my dreams too. We managed to watch and record quite a lot of memory log, but that wasn't enough. It would never be enough. I have just a glimpse of the whole story. We ahn...needed you"

The enquiry was halted by the urgent beeping coming from the other side of Doctor Anansi's office.

"Shit" Vóra spasmed. "We don't have time now. We have to go before they get to us" She raised herself, looked down at me, and raised a hand, helping me stand up too. "I don't know why we are doing all this, not really. I don't know how you managed to touch, never mind work with gravitonium like you did, and I don't know how you can help in any way. I am doing this for me and for my brother, but more than that, I am doing it because I trust your mother. If she told us to find you, well, here we are. Now let's go" She moved to the computer station by upstairs. "Donis, go with her and get the fuck out of here. I'm going to try keep them back for a while and delete her file" As she said that Adonis flipped and open his mouth to say something, but before he could, she said "I'm right behind you. Just need to do this. Go, go" She flung her hand, telling him to move. He, stuck, unmoving, looking at his sister, mouth ajar, breathed heavily, closed his eyes, and when he opened them again, there was less indecisiveness and fear, and much more resolution and intent. His mouth closed, his lips sharply shut, and his jaw clicked with tension. Not a word came from him however, not a farewell, not a jest, not a complaint. He nodded, turned around and walked fast towards the back of the room. I followed not looking back, as I would be looking at no one, because as soon as her sibling turned, she did the same, wilfully remaining behind even though the danger was crashing over us as we spoke.

***

We left Vóra behind, we were crawling and scrawling through the cilial vegetation that follows and protects the riverbanks. We haven't exchanged a single word during since we left the building, the only sounds being the farthest murmur of directions and orders being given, our lumpy and muddy steps, and the tense mouth breathing we both were pulling and pushing.

The back door dropped us out by the old pool, and

what remained of it. The aquatics complex was torn in half, and so was the pool. What was there was a dead carcass of a building, with bricks and stones hanging on metal beams and steel netting. The pool itself was also been split in two, one half still there, an empty, blue-tiled bowl, covered in green and grey lime and moss, while the other half was crater. The university had a few totems, a couple of places or monuments that would make its identity and its personality. Along with the old church and the devasted stone bridge, the aquatics complex told a story, or part of the story of the whole town. I never thought I would miss it. But then, as we crouched in the dirt, the old pool never looked so inviting and so alive.

There was a time when I would stop, sit down, and look up at the sky, seeing the light interference and how it misbehaved around and surrounding the crater. I spent many hours speculating what could have cause the incident, what were the circumstances, the results, the reactions, and why the very air passing over it and the water flowing up when it should have been falling down acted like that. From afar, one could see the clouds circling and spiralling upwards, but that close, it was a different world, one I could never and would never be comfortable.

The river ran down from west to east, from the high ground towards the larger river a few hundred miles ahead, which in its turn, would delta by the coast. Six months ago, the course of this very river was broken and halted. One of the first and most prominent projects that the foundation initiated when it started the town's renovation, was to restore the river. But, because of things I had no imagination as to what could have been before, and that later I would be able to make some sense of, the river remained. The water that came down from the west would drop and fall, and reach the bottom of the canyon, just to be elevated and pushed up, resuming its natural course on the other side.

Even then, I was fascinated with such weirdness, however unnatural it actually was in reality. After getting to know the truth of that place, for some reason, seeing the river flow upwards looked even more uncanny.

Adonis was silent for the whole journey, only announcing a hole hidden in the mud or moaning during a harder step from time to time. He returned to his less intense, calmer demeanour a behaviour I could only vouch for based on the few hours we spent together in a couple of days spread out through a few months. He looked more attentive and aware than he was the few times we spoke. Maybe because he had left his sister back at the lab, maybe because he realised that she might not meet us after all.

"Adonis" I said finally, a silence broken as the thin,

warm rain started to drop. "Should we wait for her?" I thought I should ask.

"No, not now" He didn't even looked back. "Let's get to the bridge, and then we wait. Do you know where to go?" Even though I had all the memories, he was still leading the way. Instinctively perhaps, or maybe he also knew.

I took a moment to respond. I knew I knew, but it was more like a feeling, more a call than a map. "Yes, I think I do. It's the only place that it can be."

"Good" He said that, and stood up, as we at last reached the other side of the crater site, and out of the scope of any enforcer. I followed his lead, and we both walked, stretching our legs and arms, cracking our backs and necks, towards the stone bridge leading to the other side of the river.

Adonis leaned at the short stone wall and let a heavy and long breath out. "Okay, I think we can stop for a little bit and ahn...maybe wait for my sister. If..." He stopped himself mid-sentence, bit his lips, and continued "When she gets here, we can carry on" I sat on the side of the bridge. "Are you okay?"

"Yeah" I wasn't quite sure what to say to that. "I don't know. I feel that I should be happy, or that I should be motivated, or perplexed. But the truth is that I feel lost, even more than before"

He stared at me, waiting for me to continue.

"I don't feel that I have lived all that. I have seen it and I now know that those memories are mine, and that everything that happened, actually happened. They look so...distant, so exterior. As if someone has written those stories before, and then simply glued them all on my brain and said, "here, there you go. This is you, enjoy". But in a way, that is not me, at least not me as I turned out to be. I have spent these last six months searching for what I was, and been fed lies, and been betrayed, and now that I got to see the truth, now that I got to know the real me, the me of the past, the me of the memories, I am still the me of lies, of mistrust, the me of nothing. And I don't know how to become this new thing I've been shown"

I turned to look at Adonis, but he was looking down. His mouth moved and closed again, and then he turned to me.

"You don't have to be that. You don't have to be the memories the machine showed you. Memories are not real; in a way they are stories we tell ourselves of the things another you have done in another time. Who is to say what we remember is actually the ultimate truth? I am not the person I was in my memories. In a way, I am not the same me of an hour ago. What I remember are the stories and tales that tell me of the circumstances of another moment. Postverta and Anteverta are only tools that we can use to reorganise the stories we have lost and to retell those stories as memories. You have spent all that time trying to find yourself, but you haven't. You have found a past you, of another time, of another circumstance. Now, what you can do, what you are bounded to do, is to become yourself, of now. The lines that connect us, our nature, our home, our past to ourselves now are always moving, and they are moving forward, and they are growing, always growing. So, you can choose to continue pulling this line wherever direction you want"

"You can choose to continue pulling this line". "Are you done?" I asked him. "Because I have chosen to find a line to pull all that time, and now that I have that, now that I found who I was, I am not compelled to do so. Is that bad? I don't even know if I can. I don't know it I know what to do" I climbed down the ledge and walked to the other side. Leaning down, I looked at my distorted, dysmorphic reflex on the rushed river. "We're walking for almost an hour, and I have no idea of a plan, of how to find what I need to find. I don't even know why I'm going that way. Do you?"

He was quiet for a minute. "You said you wanted to find your mother" He cut me with that. "You told us that you wanted to find her, and now that you know that she is still alive, you want to give up? I met her, you know, your mother. We all did. She was the inspiration for us all to push forward and to do what we needed to do. She was the one who found out about the foundation's projects, the gravitonium. She is the reason we are all alive now"

"I know" I said, rudely. "I saw it. With my own brain. I saw her in the lab, sending us away, going back to…" I turned away, angry with myself to be on the edge of crying in front of him, again. "I don't know if I can do it"

"My memories of her were manufactured. They weren't true" I said, more to myself than to him.

"You're wrong. Do you remember homomorphic encryption?" Adonis said as if that was an old inside joke that we both shared. "Your memories Dia, they weren't false. They have never been false. They're true. every one of them. They were simply not in the most crucial order and position. You've seen your mother as an artist and crafter. That you and her were always in her workshop, and that she gave you the knife you keep locked" As he said all that, I turned, not believing and finding all that quite natural at the same time. "I have seen that. At that millisecond, when the shard of metal hit my eyes and my sister's leg, I have shared your memories" His gaze was apologetic but constraint. He meant all that. "Our whole objective was to use gravitonium as a source of energy, to create medicine, technology, even cure diseases. But the foundation saw potential, and through potential, power. That's why we decided to end the whole project and take the source of all as far away as possible" Unknowingly, we moved closer, side by side, leaning at the bridge's ledge. "I think they found out about you, or about us all, and because of that, they decided to reinitiate their space program, and the whole Precursor stuff"

"They were baiting me. Us. They knew if they restarted the Precursor project, it would mean that they had found more gravitonium" I surprised myself with what I said. "But they didn't have any. They were waiting for me, for you and for Vóra" A worry came knocking and made me jolt. "Is Doctor Anansi...?"

"Yes. I assume so" He answered, embarrassed. "We had no idea before. We thought she was trying to help us, to find your memories, and to use the metal as we intended. But she wanted more. She wanted to be more" Adonis said that, looking down at his feet. "That's why Vóra stayed back. I realised already back there. She stayed behind to hold the Doctor back" He closed and squeezed his fists; a frustrating anger emanate from his eyes.

In my ignorance I thought I was the only one having a major shift in my reality. In my hubris, I believed everyone, and everything was plotting against me, and keeping the truth from me. In my deepest most vulnerable moment, I put myself in the centre of the universe, and thought I was special, that I was being wronged, and only me. In a moment when I needed to be charitable and open, I closed in, forged a cocoon, and held myself more important than anything else. And then, just then, when the man who showed my dreams and brought back my memories, a man who had done it before once, and that now has left his own sister back to save something bigger, I felt embarrassed for thinking I was that something bigger.

I felt a rush of cold sweat drip down my spine and my ears tingling warm. I felt dizzy, as if the bridge were collapsing out of a sudden, and the only thing stable, strong enough to hold me standing was his arm. I touched it, but he didn't look back.

"We can go back" I then said, fighting back my instinct to continue forward instead. "We can go back and wait for her. Do you want to do that?"

Adonis cleared his throat and without moving responded "We can't. Not now. Maybe earlier. Maybe I should've stayed back with her. Maybe if we had all stayed, we would've been able to escape, together. But not now. Not now, now is too late. Too late" And that was what broke him. Perhaps the knowledge that he could have been braver, that he could've acted against his older sibling's orders. And he broke down. He let his body slip down, scraping his back against the stone, he sat down, and with both hands on his face, he cried a silent cry.

I tried to say his name, I tried to find the words to comfort him, to make suffering easier, but I couldn't. I didn't know those words. I wish I did. I crouched down by him.

"I left her there, by herself" I thought he was still fighting internally with the decision he made, that he would blame himself for her...fate? But no, as he continued. "I left her there, and she send me away. She knew what we needed to do. She is giving us time, and we are wasting it" He suddenly snaps out of his monologue. "Do you know where we have to be?"

"Yes" mumbling, tripping in my own words. "Yeah, I do"

"Right, we should be there then, not here" He held my forearm, and I held his, and we both lift ourselves.

***

No memory, no image, no dream could have prepared me for that place. Since the scintillance, I hadn't been to our house, to our garden, to that time. I still had many memories of that place however, from my childhood, my early teens, the times I started thinking about moving, the thoughts about never wanting to leave. Those memories were there, always there, never lost. Those are natural, organic, I could feel that I had indeed lived through all that. I could still hear the sounds of metal beating, of the river rushing after a night of heavy rain, and the wind blowing the pine trees in mid-autumn. That was never taken from me. And even though some of them might have been broken or missing bits here and there, there was no truths truer than those memories, under the sun truths, my truths.

I was still settling and digesting the new memories, the ones handed back to me earlier. Those were not yet mine, and regardless of what anyone would say, not yet true in their final form. There was still too much conflict inside. On one side I had the memory of my mom gently teaching me how to work with metal, with fire, how to find good wood, and how to look at the neon fish. On the other side, I was trying to fit the new set of images and ideas that have emerged from the sea of emptiness my mind was right after the scintillance.

That place now looked so violated, wronged, mutilated to its core, the mutilation that follows bloodline and generations, the violation that fucks with any form of idealized dream.

The crater didn't reach the house itself, but it bent the earth under it to a point that one half had collapsed and fell on itself. The other half stood by a thread, part of it leaning over into the addend, which was mom's workshop. That hadn't moved, it remained, standing still, like the rock and stone it was made of. It was holding its ground even with the water flooding the two buildings up to my knees. It amused me that in that moment, in that situation, my mind rushing and trying to find firm ground, it still had time to compare the house and the workshop with the two states of my memory, one deplorable and falling into pieces, the other sturdy, truthful, and unmovable. Both were drowning however, which if the comparison were to be kept, I would take as a bad omen either way.

There was no more stone path, no more bench, no more settlement. I was walking on mud, then water again, struggling to move, but moving still, towards the half rotten pine door that my mom and I made ourselves. I could still see the carved pattern, the perfect ones were hers, the slightly wonky, but always improving I hoped, were mine, and our signature, two tiny letters engraved on the top corner on the inside. I walked through the threshold, even though the walls closer to the river were not there anymore. It was just natural to walk through the door.

From the inside, I could see the pine tree woods behind the house. I loved those woods and feared them almost as much. I was taught to respect the forest, to collect and to give back by the means I could conjure. We took care of the trees, and we made fire when we wanted an ancient warmth in our living room, and we made beautiful things with wood. Perhaps that was our way to give back. From the other side of the river, from town, it was difficult to see, but the trees closer to the crater were bent forward, curved from the base of the trunk, as if they were being pulled, knotted at the top, by something coming from the centre of the hole. The ones closer were brutally distorted, while the ones in the back were progressively less and less bendy. Both of us could feel that force, something gently but intently ushering us and everything else towards the crater.

Only one, the one in front of the house, the one with water covering its roots and bottom, only this one was unbent and unbroken by the force coming from the crater. It was however deformed, twisted, unsettling almost. It hasn't changed since the days I could remember and the days I couldn't. It was still half naked, bristly branches, curvy and wobbly trunk, standing on a large rock, which were now under water and mud. As the forest, I loved and feared that tree. It was there before we were, and as far as I was concerned, I hoped it stayed long after we are all gone, and these words become meaningless. There was a story my mother used to tell me about this tree, an old tale she heard from someone, but I can't recall entirely, all I know is that it had something to do with a demon and a violin.

We walked through the semi demolished rooms and crumbled walls, but nothing was there anymore, not as a house, or a memory. Eventually all the furniture got taken away or dragged down the river during a storm. Pictures were nothing more than whited out photographic paper and the curtains were eaten by moths and greened by moss. A house feels so empty when its open and vulnerable and fractured.

"Nothing here, should we go to the workshop?" I said, partly excited to see the workshop again, partly wishing to leave the house that was a home, but it was now corpse.

"Yeah, sure. Did you ahn...find anything?" Adonis asked, sounding less distressed than before.

"No, not yet. I can feel it's here somewhere, but I don't have an image to follow or a map. It's just a sense, a very vague sense that I know where it is" I replied moving quickly, familiar with the movement I had to do in the water, towards the stone building at the other end of the property.

"It's just, very cold" Adonis complaint.

It was midday or closer to it, and the sun was hidden behind thick clouds, only visible through the hole in the clouds above the crater. It was terribly cold, but I choose to embrace it. It was keeping me aware and sharp, but now that he brought that up, it was indeed terribly cold. The workshop was dark, damp, and echoey, creating an odd fluidity in the reverberation of our steps and voices.

I turned to the left of the door and grabbed

the desk I knew was still there to direct myself through the room. Adonis went to the other side, following the east wall. The light was sparse and obnoxiously faint, only giving away the slightest edges of objects and furniture. I heard him touching things, stepping over tools, and cursing under his breath.

"You alright? Don't hurt yourself" I joked. "There're a lot of tools and equipment back there, so be careful"

"What are we looking for again?" he said. "Not that it would matter much, I can't see anything"

"I can't see shit also. And I don't know what we're looking for. I just know it's here and I know it's close" I tried to sound as serious as I could, so he wouldn't think I was joking that time.

I only heard a faint, distant "okay" coming from the other side, and the clumsy stepping and tripping resumed.

I knew that workshop as the palm of my hand and knew I could thread my way through its tight space with my eyes closed. But there I was, with eyes wide open and not seeing anything, and my hands by my side and not recognising those lines, not anymore, not yet.

The scar never actually hurt before. I couldn't place the time I got it even. I assumed it was during the time of the incident, maybe debris, maybe an accident. I asked about it just once, and once I was told I had always had it. But that was just another lie. That was part of the new memories, the ones that I did just get, not my old, familiar, lived ones. I never asked again, and it never bothered me. It never hurt, it never ached, it never scratched, at least not different from any other part of the body when those scratches. Until now.

It started as a thin pain, as paper cut. The pain grew and grew, and began to feel as it was opening, pulled from all sides of my chest, that it was trying to pull it apart and break my skin.

"Wow, do you have a light there? I though you've left your pad back there in the office. It's not safe to have it here with us Dia" Adonis said that, and the sound came muffled by the pain and by the weirdness of the question. Light, which light? My eyes were closed, and I was struggling to stand, so I shift my weight and seated in the broken chair I had my hand on.

He might have heard me moan and swear, because the next thing I felt was his hand on my shoulder. "Are you okay? What's happening? Why do you have your pad with you?"

"What" I said between the cramps in my chest. "Are you saying?" I felt the rushing of the waves of pain crawling and snagging my skin, pulsating and actioning the nerves around the scar. "I don't have it"

I opened my eyes, because he didn't reply and because the waves of discomfort were getting smaller and smaller every second now. And the blue light coming from the inside of my shirt, from the scar, was so bright that the whole room was now existing in this single hue. It was so strong and so powerful, that it made me forget about the pain, or the pain stopped. I wasn't sure.

My scar was flooding the room with this intense blue as I managed to regain my strength, and the pain was just a past life away. Adonis didn't know how to act, so he didn't, he just stayed put, kneeling by the chair where I was sitting.

I had to see what was happening, what was creating this light. I even questioned myself if I had in fact left my pad back at the office or not. But I had, I knew I had. It wasn't that. I took my jacket off, turned around, with my back to Adonis, the light now hitting the back of the room. I unbuttoned my shirt, and I could then see. The scar tissue was gleaming like a neon sign, lightly flickering, and from the centre, through what it has been the original cut in my chest, a direct light emanated as floodlights, blue floodlights. I touched the skin, and the pain resumed. Not bad as before, more as a straining of muscles after a run, as if my innards were working some sort of peculiar digestion of some sort.

From inside of the scar something was pushing out. I could see a bump forming, and I could feel something moving from within, fighting to break out. It wasn't however just a push from the inside, but I could also feel a pull from something or somewhere from outside. Something in that room was pulling me towards it.

My mind began to spin violently, a whirlpool of memories and images flashing through my eyes, of things that had taken place in the workshop. I saw myself in the middle, and many people, some that I knew, some unfamiliar or unknown, walking fast by and around me. I could see myself down there, struggling with the pain, surrounded by blue light. I saw another figure moving as well. Not me, not Adonis, a figure of memory. Chris.

I held something in my hand, something sharp and shiny. I was gesticulating and arguing apparently, and so did he, but I couldn't hear my own words, the light was too loud. I presented the item, perhaps pointing at him, as he came closer and closer, and grabbed my hand. We appear to have reached an agreement, but out of nowhere, he turned the blade towards me. I tried to hold it back, pushed him away, but he was stronger. I was watching myself fighting him to no aval, the blade had a path, and it was moving towards its goal. Even from the ceiling looking down at the two of us, I felt the cold sting of the sharp edge starting to cut my skin, the fractal pain travelling quickly taking the breath out of my lungs, while the warm red blood spilt in thin red lines at first, then a larger, deeper river. The pain was the reverse of what I felt minutes before. The strain from outside to inside, skin breaking, muscles breaking, bones cracking. I couldn't hold that any longer, my sight was getting blurred, and I stopped breathing altogether. With a final push, Chris penetrated the knife in my heart, and the lights were out.

Not Dia in the ceiling, I looked at my hands, now in the darkness again, and didn't see nor feel any blood. I thought that whole thing, the light, Chris, the knife, was only a dream. Maybe that didn't actually happen, maybe it was some kind of misinterpretation happening between my old and new memories, that were making up fantasy scenarios, trying to figure out how to live together in the same brain. For a moment I was content with that reality, happy that both the light and the pain stopped.

And for the third time that day, the pain returned, stronger and more precise than before. The push and the pull were ripping me apart. No light this time, I was shouting and crying in the dark dampness of the workshop once again. I could feel my body letting go, all the fibres of my skin being torn apart and crushed, and at the point I believed I would pass out because of the agony, a shard of light opened again in the form of my scar, and through it came water, and blood, and something else. I held the object coming out of me from no-where inside of my body and pulled. Pulled and shouted and cried and finally it came out. More water and more blood poured out before the light ceased and the scar closed, as if had never hurt before.

There was nothing there anymore. It was just my-self, kneeling down, my face bloated and my eyes red, my nose dripping and my hair loose and wet. I could feel myself gripping the knife, still under the water that covered the whole workshop.

"Dia!?" I forgot about Adonis. "What happened? What happened with the light?"

I wanted to say, "I don't know", but I couldn't say anything. After what I have hurt, what I have felt, what I have remembered, I shouted instead.

***

Darkness turned to light, a blue light that shone from my own body. I could see myself in that memory, I was living that memory. The floor was not drowning anymore, the hearth was still warm, the tools recently used, and me, holding the knife I had just attached to the blade I had forged and beaten just hours ago at the foundation's labora-tory. The light wasn't coming from me after all, it was coming from the waves of blue gravitonium lodged into steel. I was holding the handle firmly, binding the glue and securing the silver rods that were keeping the blade in place. "We have to hide this thing Chris" I said without talking, "they can't find it". As I said that I noticed that in fact Chris was there, in front of me, but far. How could I have not noticed before? He was silent, distant, not re-acting to what I was saying. "Yes", he finally said, or at least the sound of his voice came from his dir-ection, "this cannot stay here". A vague statement, and not exactly an answer to my worries. In a blink of the eye, he was too close to me, staring with vacant eyes at something that was behind me, far away. "I'm sorry" he then said, and I felt his hands holding mine, forcing them upwards. I tried to hold him, but I wasn't that strong. "Bring the metal back, and you'll have your father", but it wasn't his voice, it was someone else's, someone I knew and have heard before, but couldn't see a face. The blue gleam got stronger, brighter, and then I felt it being pushed inside me. I looked down to my chest, and saw the blade passing through my body, drove in its entirety, blade, guard, and handle. The light disappeared, as did everything else. I felt the breeze outside, being carried, felt the water of the river embrace and engulf my whole body, and the water fill all the openings of my body. The air in my lungs was pulled out, and I tried to bring it back in.

**

I woke up gasping for air, exasperatedly inhaling

as fast and as hard as I could, trying to grasp back to this reality. The air came burning down my throat and my nose, down my lungs and stomach, my chest bursting with the sudden inner pressure, even my ribcage clicked and cracked, expanding to a point of exploding. But it didn't. I was alive, hurt, stabbed by my best friend, wet, and in the dark, but alive.

My body was heavy, so I let it fall back, expecting to be met with the cold water on my neck and shoulders, but I was stopped, held. Adonis was looking down at me, worried, confused surely, and I could only say "I found it", as I lifted the naked blade from the water, still tightly gripped in my right hand.

***

ON BECOMING

We sat down for an hour, talking about the day behind us, about the memories that have been reconnecting with the old ones, and understanding what to do with the thing I had pulled out of my chest, through a scar that opened to nowhere inside my body, and how I was stabbed and left to die by my best friend.

"I've seen all that, I could feel all that happening with me just there, but I know that those are things of the past, memories that were brought back because of this thing" I was still holding the blade. The handle was missing, so I grasped the metal tang, enjoying the cool metal touch. "He drove this thing inside of me, and it was there this whole time, but not really" I didn't believe even as I was saying it.

"I'm not going to ask if you're sure. I ahn...believe that you have seen whatever you have seen" Adonis was silent for some time. "I just hope that what you've learned can help us"

"So do I" I smiled a reply, thinking about his sister.

She hadn't come nor contacted us in any way. I'd never expected the worse, but after learning what I'd learned that day, I knew that what we were after, what we found, was more important than we believed it to be.

And Chris. It felt hard to talk about then, to see that happening with me for a second time, because as I was speaking, retelling the betrayal, the murder, it was becoming more real. Just as I dreamed, I would discuss and go through what I had seen with Carrie, I did the same thing with Adonis then. Without mints, in the open, watching the sun moving behind the orange, grey and silver clouds. We climbed up in the workshop's roof to get away from the water that was becoming colder and to maybe be able to see further, beyond the river and the bridge, just at the edge of the pathway to the town. "We can stay up here and check when she gets close" I told him, maintaining the hope that Vóra was fine, and it would be simply a matter of time for her to arrive.

"She'll probably be very angry with you when she gets here" I played with him, even though I couldn't know if what I was saying was true. I hoped so.

"She will" He chuckled but didn't smile. "She can be quite, ahn..."

I filled the void "Scary?"

"Yeah" A more sincere laugh. "She definitely can be very scary. But she is just trying to protect me. For over twenty years, she always thought she needed to protect me. And now, I really think that maybe she was right" He sighed deeply. "And I couldn't protect her. In the end, she was right"

The wind got stronger and cooler, and I could few thin drops of water slicing through my face. "Maybe she is right. She did protect you and me. And then you protected me, all the way here, all the way to this thing" I didn't know if I was trying to make him feel better or if I was worrying myself about the same thing.

That discussion died off after a minute. "What you'll do with that? Do you know how to use it?" Adonis pointed at the naked knife in my hand. "Did you know it was inside of you?"

"No. I don't think it was at all inside of me actually. It was only when I was at that exact spot inside that the whole memory came back and this thing...appeared" I was still figuring out myself how to come to terms with it. It looked, it felt as if it came from my scar, from within me. "I don't know how to explain, but I don't believe the knife was inside of me, but it needed to pass through me. I was not its vessel, I was a threshold" Or more specifically my scar was, and that exact spot was the hole in the wall, and I was the door.

"I see" He felt resolute with the response, even though it wasn't at all an explanation. Adonis then continued. "We were studying gravitonium for a long time. We, my sister and I, were looking at its behaviour as a particle and we tried to apply the concept of homomorphic encryption into it. We broke it in two and separate them. We discovered that when we moved one, the other would follow. We could even surpass the paradox and measure its trails and trajectories without collapsing the whole entanglement system. The foundation funded this research and patented its results. It was found later that graviton was too unpredictable to work with, so we thought it would be a good idea to artificially alter its state, and radioactive it" He lectured as he did before, in his office, the first time we spoke. "During this process, we created gravitonium, and stabilised into a metal rod. And when we thought we struck gold, in the middle of the room, just like your scar, that blue light shone all over us, and through a cut in the air, something came through"

I felt myself gripping the blade as if someone were trying to take it away from me. I felt my ears burning and my jaw click and noticed I wasn't breathing. I pull back the air and filled my chest. "What did?"

Adonis looked much older in that light. Not physically, but his eyes, they looked like old eyes, eyes that had seen things, good things, and bad too.

A terrifyingly heavy and distressed eye. Grey eyes with just the smallest glint of blue.

"A piece of metal. Old metal, of centuries past. Space grade metal, with a trademark and ID code tracking back to the Precursor" he finished that as an omen.

"And what does that mean?" I questioned, not sure of how much of the answer I would be able to absorb.

"Not much in itself. But in the context of the larger things, in the trials and errors of experiment, we brought back instantly a piece of a spacecraft millions of lightyears and hundreds of years away" My face might had been a clean slate of emotions and reaction, because Adonis decided to give the explanation another go. "I ahn...how to explain? It's lightspeed"

"Ah, I get it. So, this metal and the experiment created a lightspeed transport? And that brought back a piece of that ship? Is that it?" I asked, managing the best scientific explanation an Anthropology graduate could give.

"Ahn, no, not actually" He smiled, not a funny or sarcastic smile, but a fulfilled, satisfied one. "We didn't achieve lightspeed Dia, we made it irrelevant"

Irrelevant. Such a word to describe lightspeed.

Movies, media, books, they all put such a great deal of attention and awe into the concept of faster than light travel; quantum physics, avionics, astrophysics, all of them have at their most unachievable goal to reach a velocity so as to surpass that of light itself. And now, with forged gravity, humanity has made sure that this all-encompassing, everlasting impossible milestone was…irrelevant.

As I started to open my mouth and query Adonis more on how I made a knife out of universe bending material, I've heard the furious, fast, and heavy steps ruffling the leaves and mud. The steps came from the bridge, from the other side of the river. And with the steps, came a voice, a familiar voice, a voice I rejoice to hear months ago, after an eternity without that sound next to me. A voice that left me when I didn't have anything, and then came back swearing it would help me this time. A voice that took me to my dear friend, only for her to leave and die. A voice that told me in my ears, while stabbing me with my own blade, that I needed to die. That voice, shouting my name.

"Dia!" the blurred that was Chris running was coming closer. His voice was loud regardless his visible straining and tiredness. He might have been running the whole way from Mal's place for the looks of it. "Dia!" He shouted again, stepping in the muddy water and stopping, finally having a chance to breath. And deep breathes he took, making me both curious and impatient.

Holding the blade, I stepped up, standing on the roof, looking down at him, trying my best to show discomfort, wearing my best menacing façade. "What are you doing here?" I enunciated every word as sharp and as accusing as I knew how to. Every word a wound.

"Dia, I...I woke up at...your friend's home... couch...and you weren't there...I didn't know where you were, so I went out...ran out" He was still puffed, collecting droplets of air between his words. "I went to the foundation because I thought you might have been there still. But the whole place was surrounded by people and enforcers...so I tried...this place"

I looked down at Adonis, and then at him, measuring what my mind and my heart were telling me to do. I should never know which one convinced me first, but I climbed down the roof, blade still in hand, and met him face to face.

"You" He was looking at it. He knew exactly what it was. "You found it? How? I...It was..." Anything he said would be wrong.

I didn't help him complete the sentence. I wanted to make him realise that I also knew what had happened. I wanted him to feel the anger brewing inside of me.

"Dia. How did you find it? Where was it?" He was more interested in knowing where it was than anything else. "We were looking for it for so long. Isn't it right, Adonis?" They both finally meet eyes. Adonis was now next to me, looking straight in front, claiming his position.

"Yes. We were looking for it. All of us" Adonis sounded scared, even though he was modulating his voice, trying to appear stronger.

"That's great Dia. That's so good. Now we can finally continue working on the metal. I mean, that was what our parents were doing all those years. We have to go and continue what they began" He was being someone else. His voice I knew, but the words coming from it, they were premade, rehearsed, given to him. "Dia, come with us, we can help you"

"Who is 'us'?" I snapped finally. "Why did you come?"

"Why?" Puzzled, he shrugged. "What do you mean? I came to help you, to help you find your memories, help you find this" He pointed at the knife, accusatory and possessive. "Can I see it?"

He started to walk to where I was. I made sure to put myself in between him and my blade. His eyes were piercing, poking me, questioning my moves.

"What's wrong Dia?" He asked, as if either he didn't know or was pretending not to know. I didn't know him anymore. I knew him as a kid, as children, as teenagers, and briefly partially through adulthood, but not this person. His face, his eyes, the scar I left on his face, they were all the ones I knew, but his presence, that wasn't my friend anymore. "Let me help you with that. Let me hold it for you" He reached out to me, hands moving in my direction, eyes locked on mine, aiming at the knife.

I paced back a step, reacting to him coming closer. Repugnance more than fear, a disgust for what he had done.

"Dia, hand me the knife, please. What are you doing? I came all the way here to help you, don't you see? I came back because of you, because I wanted to be with you again. I'm sorry I wasn't there for you when you needed someone, but look, I'm here, I'm back, and we can use that to make everything right again" He was nervous, his mouth betrayed him spilling too many words. I stepped back one more step, protecting the blade with my other hand. He snapped "Fuck Dia! What the fuck you think you're doing? Give me this fucking thing now! I need that, now!" And then, he gave himself away.

I kept my stand, but he, hearing back what he has just said, the way he said, he threw his hands down, his head back, and moan loudly, giving up the acting. He brought his head back down, his arms loose by his side, he took three deep, long breathes, licked his lips, and looked up at me. "Dia, you have to give this thing to me right now. I need that. I need to use that to bring my dad back" He swallowed and his demeanour changed, from aggressive to bargaining. "We can use to bring your mom back too. Right? Isn't that what you want too? We can bring both of them back. I...we. We just need to hand the knife back to them, and they'll use to bring them both back to us. Isn't that good?" His patronising tone sent shivers down my spine and boiled the blood in my hearth.

"Who are they?" I snarled back at him.

"They. The foundation, Dia, who else? They know what to do, they can take care of it" He shouted back. "We can leave it to them, and we can just go. Go and be free of it"

"And let them blow everything up? Don't you remember what Carrie said about this thing?" I reminded him.

He seemed puzzled for a moment. After a few seconds, as if finding the correct answer, he said. "Fuck Carrie. She's gone. She lied to you Dia, she knew all that and more, and didn't tell you. Didn't tell me either" He was right about it. "She didn't care about you" But he was wrong about that.

It felt as if I needed time to assess that statement, but I didn't. I knew what I had to do; I just couldn't bring myself to do it. "I can't. I won't" I resolved.

His eyes turned white, his hands tense turned into fists, and his teeth clenched and gritted in anger. "I need this fucking knife! And I will take if from you if I have to Dia"

"As you tried to do before? When you killed me, and threw me in the river?" I said, calmer than I thought I could ever be. "You lost the knife that time, and you won't have it now"

Nothing else was said. The silence fell and we drowned under it. He started to lose control, pacing and rubbing his face and chin, finding movements that would keep his limbs occupied while his brain dealt with my dismissal. I have never seen him acting like this. He was always calm around me. But not then.

"Why did you do that?" the sentence left my mouth as a croak.

His eyes met mine with anger and despair. He was about to answer my question, but as he opened his mouth, he turned back, scanning for something we couldn't hear or see yet. He didn't move and kept staring at the stone bridge connecting the town with the flooded woods and the other side of the river. The bridge that was suddenly populated by two cars, white and silver, with the foundation's emblem etched on their sides and tops.

"She's here" Chris said, scared again, and without looking at me continued. "I'm sorry Dia"

***

The two cars stopped abruptly, spilling the mud, before stopping just before the water line in the small, flooded peninsula. All doors opened, and from one of them a white-coat, wild-hair Doctor Anansi jumped out of the car, with an undiscerning look on her face, she came towards us three, but mostly towards me. She stopped and looked for a second, caught her breath and analysed the situation, looking from me to Adonis, then to Chris, then the knife, then me again. A smile then draw lines around her mouth and eyes and at the base of her nose. She opened her arms, as if waiting for a hug from an old friend, and suddenly dropped then on her sides, letting the air scape her.

"Dia, finally, we found you Dia. Where were you, girl?" Then she addressed Adonis "And you two, we were looking for you both too" She said that, still smiling. "You didn't show up for the tests Dia. What was wrong? I thought he would make you change your mind, with the whole '*protecting you and making sure you did only what you wanted*' little speech. That didn't work, no" She had her hands clenching her waist, obviously not happy, but the smile remained. "I told you it wouldn't work Adonis" I looked at him, feeling betrayed again. Losing the count of how many times.

"It's not like that Dia" He mumbled, trying to manage the full range of emotions and thoughts going through his head. And failing at that.

"No Dia, it is not like that" Anansi took the reply and went with it. "It was not supposed to be like that. We, you and me, were supposed to work together" Her voice was louder and more distressed. She noticed that and stopped. Her hands met palm to palm, and she brought this pair to rest in front of her face, touching her lips, eyes closed, but moving, attentive. "I'm sorry Dia. I thought you would care about what we were doing. That's why I brought you in, that I told you things you didn't know, and you told me about your dreams" She filled her chest with the fresh air of that afternoon and expelled it loudly. "I want to help you Dia"

I was about to reply, to say that I didn't need any help, that I have been offered help already, but she was faster.

"He offered you help already?" Pointing at Chris.

I didn't answer. Yes, he had offered me help, and yet I refused.

"Of course he did. Did he say how is he going to help? No right? Yes, I didn't think so" she walked back to one of the cars and leaned on his side. "He can't help you Dia. He doesn't have anything that can help you my dear. Do you know why he is here?" I looked at her, then at him, but no answer came from my old friend. "Well, that's a little sad. He is here because I ask him to. He came back because he ran away before, and I made him come back. I asked him to come to you" The surprise must have been too visible in my eyes, because she twitched and smiled. "That's funny. You still thought he came for you. Not everything revolves around you. But somethings do" She lift herself and kept walking, reaching just enough to have her shoes wet at the tip. "I want to be very clear with you Dia, so you understand what I am saying. I need that knife you have there, and you friend there was kind enough to suggest that he would help you find it and then make you hand it over to me. I know, it sounds foolish as I say it too. But, even as farfetched as that sounded, it was an opportunity that fell on my lap, courtesy of our beloved Carrie, who arranged it all" Every word, every sentence, every new information she gave, effortlessly made me feel more gullible. "But I assume you figured it all out already. If not, there you have it" She moved again, pacing from one side to the other. "There was just one thing that unfortunately I didn't foresee. Carrie was a real asset, and in the end, she gave in, wanting to preserve a moment for an eternity" She took a tin box from her coat, the mint box I was so familiar, opened it and after second closed it again with a click. "In any case, of course, I wouldn't let that on his hands alone. No, I had my marvellous assistants" She thrust her open palm faced up in Adonis's direction. "Who, as I found too much too late, have been doing their own side projects behind my back" She turned back, facing the cars, the river, the crater, and the foundation far in the background. "This crater is so full of energy, can you feel? It pulls us into it. Is so subtle, but so, so strong. All the weather, the clouds, the trees even, are all drawn to this epicentre. And we had that in our hands. We had that, right there, that I could grab it"

She turned again. "Dia, I was wrong. I thought that by manipulating or deceiving you I would be able to bring it back. But that was wrong. I was wrong. I am sorry if I put you in a situation you didn't want to be. And I am also sorry Chris, for making you go after your friend and lie to her. And Adonis, I am sorry for not giving you and your sister the independence and respect you deserved" Vóra. My mind spun back a few hours, hearing her shouting at me. I could only imagine what Adonis was feeling.

"Where is she?" He asked, his voice a rasp, air passing through clenched teeth.

"Oh yes. I am sorry. Open up" Anansi gestured to one of her security personnel and promptly the back door of the car Anansi was in opened, and they pulled Vóra out.

"Vóra!" Adonis shouted. The enforcer held her by the arm until she was out of the car, but as soon as she could stand properly, she claimed it back, furious face staring at Anansi, as if stares could kill.

Adonis wanted to move, to run towards then. But I held him back, put my arm, the one holding the blade, in front of him, blocking his way. He looked at me, and I just said quietly "wait".

"She is here Adonis. Sound and safe, as if I would have her, or any of you hurt for no particular reason" She claimed.

"What do you want?" I wanted to know.

"Want? You know what I want Dia. I told you already. The knife, that is what I want. That, however, has nothing but mere coincidence to do with my assistant here" She moved towards Vóra, looked at the enforcers and gestured for them to leave and let her go. "Vóra, I am also very sorry. I hoped we could have parted ways in better terms" Her arm made a horizontal arch, showing a free and cleared path from there to myself and Adonis. "As I said, I told them what I need, and I don't want to coerce you, I want to convince you. So, you can go now, I said I was bringing you to your brother, and that is what I am doing" But as Vóra looked away, and started moving, Anansi, as if remembering something exclaimed "However!" And Vóra stopped. "I do need to keep what belongs to me, to the foundation, before you leave us Vóra"

"What are you...?" Vóra didn't finish her question, as she felt the heavy hands of two enforcers holding her by the arms. "What the fuck is this? What are you doing?"

Adonis pushed my arm down and set off, running to his sister. He was too focused on her, too tunnel vision, that he didn't notice a third enforcer coming on his right. He grabbed Adonis by his shirt and pinned him down, making him drown in the shallow pool where we were standing. Anansi however had her eyes on Vóra the whole time.

"Your brother was hit by those fragments, right in his eyes, barely a scratch, but gave him a few quite interesting abilities, dreams of memories, even if a scarce few" She reached her pocket again, for the tin of mints, and grabbed a single pill, and gave it to Vóra. "Here, take this" Vóra was probably fighting the idea to act upon that, to react, to do something, something physical, something to hurt the Doctor perhaps. But twice she looked at her brother, held down by the large man, and twice she turned her head to confront the woman, the Doctor, and the pill. She took it. "Now Vóra here, she was also hit. But by a whole piece, a shard of the metal, that is allocated in her leg. It's annoying, isn't it? It hurts when you walk sometimes? I am sure it does. But, as I said, I am here for the knife, and I am here to help".

Vóra had her gaze fixed on the Doctor. A controlled fury. But she gave up the gaze, and instead frowned, in discomfort, in pain. She started to gnarl, and breath heavily, and scream. "These mints, they are fascinating. We made a variety of them, using some of the essence of gravitonium. Some of them make memories and dreams more vivid, especially the ones caused by the scintillance" Anansi pointed at Dia. "Some create a state of stasis, particularly useful for long, century-long trips. And others – these ones - we developed as a mining tool. You see, we used a reverted polarity of the gravitonium, which makes the user an anti-gravitonium mechanism, pushing it out of hard-to-find places. We expected to use them if we ever found mines of Gravitonium...that didn't happen, yet at least. But those mints help oust gravitonium nuggets" Vóra was still suffering, Adonis still on the ground, secured by the enforcer, and Chris still immobile. "Such as what Vóra here is experiencing" Vóra dropped down on her knees and fell on her side. Her thigh, the one with the limp, began to grow and appeared to be pulling up by an invisible arm. Adonis's sister screamed a last, devastating scream, as her leg cracked open, ripping her trousers, and pushing her away.

There was silence for a moment. Vóra laid down, barely conscient, moaning quietly in the mud, next to the crooked tree. Adonis managed to escape the grip of the man, who got distracted after what had just happened, and ran over to his sister. And I couldn't believe what I was seeing, again, for the second time this day, a piece of metal, of blue sheen and glow, expelled, birthed from inside of a person. First herself, and now Vóra. I moved, slowly, to where Adonis had her in his arms.

"And here it is. The piece that was missing, inside of you this whole time. Just like yours Dia" And she turned to us three. "Yours however, much more elegant than...that" She held the bloodied and muddied piece of metal in her hands, reaching for a handkerchief to clean it.

***

We managed to lift Vóra and take her to the stones surrounding the old tree, the only place not drowned. I ripped my jacket and managed enough fabric for a makeshift torniquet to secure her leg and stop the bleeding. It was horrible to look, and impossible to forget. Such violence, for what?

I tried to talk to her, but she was in pain. We wrapped her leg and left her there, supported by the rest of my jacket and Adonis' jumper. "She'll be okay. We can take her home and take a look at the wound later" I tried to ease the situation. I was propping myself to rise, trying not to fall from the irregular stones, when I saw Adonis fast walking furiously from where his sister was propelled.

"Adonis" I yelled.

He didn't listen. Instead, he stomped his way through the water and mud, and the enforcers, who were told to let him be by the Doctor. Adonis didn't care, maybe not even noticed her dismissing her security while he approached. He finally got to her and grabbed by her collar. Words didn't come out of his mouth, but his stare spoke plenty. Doctor Anansi, however, was unaffected. Her face was calm and settled.

"Adonis, what are you going to do? Hit me? Kill me maybe? I didn't want to kill her, but she had something that belonged to me, and for that I did, unfortunately, hurt your sister. And I am sincerely sad that I had to do it. But you see" She touched his hands with hers, and slowly made him loose his grip and let her go. "She lied to me. You both did. I didn't know her limp was because of the accident Adonis. I found out later, much later. Too late perhaps, to be able to move on and try to trust you two again" She handed the metal to one of her personnel. "But I am not a monster. I am simply doing what I must, what is needed. We have put too much effort and too much energy into this place, to let everything fall apart at the very end"

I stood next to Adonis; my eyes also fixed on her. "And to whom you are going to answer when you blow up the whole foundation again? When you blow up the whole town?"

She turned, a grin. And then she laughed. A heavy, loud laugh. "To whom I am going to answer? My dear, you don't know the half, no, a tenth of what is happening here. I don't answer to anyone. After the scintillance took part of the town and cracked the earth, the higher ups, the real foundation higher ups, decided to kill it out. No witnesses, no facts, no history. Because of you and your friends' antics back then, all the people in town became no more than collateral. I didn't let them do it. I forced my hand so the foundation would invest in reconstructing what was destroyed. I requested funds from the space project, so that money and support could make this place prosper again" She then stopped for a moment, visibly emotional, nothing like as I had seen her before. "I told them I was going to make things right again, that the research on gravitonium was valuable, that it could indeed be used along the Precursor project" Calmer now, she moved closer. "I don't answer to anyone in this place. And I will make this work" Her finger pointing directly to my nose.

She turned back and walked away. "This will have to do. Let's go" And the enforcers climbed back to their respective cars.

"Wait" Chris finally snapped out of his paralysis. I forgot he was still there. "Wait! What about the knife? Don't you need the knife? You said…"

Anansi paused, touched her temple and rubbed slowly. "You're still here Chris? Yes, you are right, I do need the knife. And you do need it as well, much more than I do if I'm not mistaken. You see Dia, he came all this way, just to get it from you.

Coming back here wasn't his idea. No, it was mine, with Carrie's help of course. I told him that if I could have the blade, I could possibly try to bring his own father back. And yes, that is true, I could. But the problem is..." And one more time, she turned to face all of us. "Your mother Dia, she was smart. Very smart. She knew that it wouldn't be enough to simply steal the metal and take it away. No, the metal needed to be worked, it needed... how can I put it...to be alive, and to receive life from a maker, from you" She gestured at me. "The metal has a kind of personality, a curious affection for its maker. When Chris tried to take it from you and tried to kill you, he failed. Because the blade is obedient and loyal, so it hid itself in you instead. I realised that when I got here. I knew that it could not be controlled, so I reached for the second-best option, the shard in Vóra's leg".

Chris' eyes were twitching, fear mixed with despair and anger. "So, I'm sorry again Chris. You did what I asked you to do, and in your way, you tried your best, but no, now I won't be able to save your father, nor Dia's mother" As she finished her last word, Chris advanced, in a possessed sprint, with the Doctor as his goal, his victim, his prey. We were audience to that, simply watching the whole thing unfolding. And impotently, I watched Chris be held by the arm, twisted, and then broken, and have his head held by one of the enforcers hands, and pushed, thrusted into the earth. Water, mud, and blood burbled and floated as he spasmed one single time, one last time. "I'm sorry Chris" Doctor Anansi opened the door and looked back at where the three of us were standing, petrified. "You have an important artefact with you Dia. I have mine as well. I hope you find good use of yours, as I will try to do of mine. Your mother, she is still out there, in another life perhaps. We'll never know". Those were the last words I heard from the Doctor, and I would see her one more time before the end.

We watched as the cars spun their wheels, finding the grip in the mud, and disappearing in the turn just before the bridge.

***

ON REACHING

I brought the last blood-soaked cloths and clothes to the washing area where Mal was already cleaning. We spent hours fitting and sterilizing Vóra's leg, until the blood stopped flowing out, and she fell asleep. She was pale, drained in both body and mind. The slash looked worse outside, with all the dirt and mud, but the impact was big and deep enough, breaking her femur. We carried her at night, through woods, by the river, until we got to the block of apartment buildings where I was living, and where I would have seen my friend, my old friend for the last time. I thought about Chris all the way. These memories crossed my mind, visions of things we had been through, times of us playing, of love and of friendship, of both those things lost in a craze of despair. I could still see myself asking for forgiveness after I marked his face with the glowing hot metal. He never said "I'm sorry", but he did then. Maybe not to me, maybe to himself, to his father. All through the whole way I shared the weight of Vóra with

Adonis, and carried the heaviness of loss.

Adonis also had much to think and to reflect. His sister, his work, his mentor, their own particular connection with the metal, consequently with me as well. I didn't want to come between him and his thoughts, so I kept quiet, thinking my own thoughts. I could have said something, I just didn't know what.

And Vóra was alive, in pain, and pain creating hallucinations and fever. Her eyes were empty, the white prominently taking over her pupils, and dark, full bags under her orbits. Her lips were cracked, dry blood mixed with the saliva, from time to time made her cough, a cracked, raspy cough. The only thing I thought pertinent to say to her was "we are almost there, hang on for just a little longer, we are almost there". She didn't say anything. I thought a nod she did was an answer, but it could have just been her head bobbing because of our awkward carrying. "We are almost there", I said, to myself too.

Mal promptly helped us lay Vóra on the couch. Things were thrown on the floor, she ordered me around, and I obeyed. I brought the old sheets, the water, the medicine, the liquor. The hours passed like centuries, and those centuries like seconds. We sat down on the carpet, in silence, watching Adonis' sister sleeping, breathing, alive.

I gave Mal the red tinted cloth. "I'm sorry Mal. I should've…"

She turned, her round face looked less round, bonier and emptier, but she was smiling, softly, mostly with her eyes. "Oh hon…yes, maybe you should have. But you didn't, and that is past" She turned back and continued washing "We might have been good friends Dia, you know that? If you haven't, you know, been gone for so long. If nothing of that hullabaloo had happened. Maybe… right?"

That could have been truth, but we'll never know "Yes, absolutely Mal. We could have been really good friends" I wished I had phrased it differently "We are friends. Thank you"

She turned again quickly, her eyes letting just the smallest tear drop. I touched her in the shoulder, and pulled myself out, back to the living room.

Adonis had his head on his sister's feet, looking at her sleep, himself fighting to stay awake. They both have put themselves at risk, so we could find the blade. For the first time since we started walking slowly back from the house, the workshop, the crooked tree, I couldn't feel the coldness and sharpness of the knife. I felt connected to it, as if it were part of my body, as if it were made not just by me, but of me, through me, and through myself it was born. For a moment I felt lost, tense, unease for not having the metal touching my skin. I turned my head side by side, looking, scanning the room.

"It's in your room Dia. You left it there" A tired, defeated voice announced the good news to me. He didn't have the energy to stand or even turn to me.

"Are you okay?" I asked, trying to hide my concern for the knife. "Do you want anything to eat, to drink?"

He cleaned is throat "No, I need to be here with her. It's all good" And he closed his eyes, pushing away a heavy breath, and falling asleep. I pushed the blanket and covered him, and quietly I said, "Thank you", and forced myself to rest as well.

With major relief I found the knife, reflecting the fading light from the living room, laying on my bed. For a moment it felt as it was glowing again, but if it was, it was gone as quickly as it came.

***

Weeks have passed, and no news from the foundation's sudden enforcer invasion, no officially announced motives, the headlines reading only "Routine evacuation test" and "Security systems put in place for the progress of the space program". I went back to the office one more time. The old church, our office, raided and breached. Files, paper, machines on the floor, the electricals unwired, all dimly lit by the gentle ink of the windows driving the light from outside. I followed the particles of dust for a moment, rising from chaos. Anti-gravity. If felt almost ironic that this was the only part of the university that stood after the scintillance.

I wasn't sure why I decided to go back at all. There was nothing there for me anymore. Just to see it again, for what it would be the last time. Quick shivers ran up my neck and ears when the glass doors on the other side of the room opened suddenly. I didn't move and waited. "Good morning," shouted the elderly man. Tall and strong looking, he held a large bucket, full of water by the swing of it, and a broom, and headphones covering his ears and his balding head. I nodded and said "Good morning" back to him.

Adonis, Vóra, and I were together for the first time since the day after I found my knife. We have all received the notification on our pads. An announcement would be made in the evening of the thirty first, which would be revealing the next steps of the foundation's space project, SEEK, featuring its head director, Doctor Anansi.

***

Good morning all. My name is Doctor Anansi, I am the lead designer, project leader and head director at the ARIA foundation. We have unprecedented news to offer you. Recently we have had a quantum leap in our space project research and development. As of today, unexpectedly, we have achieved the optimum scenario to initiate our tests for the final form of our SEEK program. We are happy to announce that adding to SEEK, we can now unveil the next level of our program, the Precursor. The Precursor was the very first research and development project fully designed within our laboratories, centuries ago. As of the first of the seventh, at two after peak noon, we will engage our first full test of the newly rebranded SEEK-Precursor program. We are delighted to announce this fascinating new chapter in ours and our town's life.

From all members of the ARIA foundation. Thank you.

***

In the day and time stated in the announcement, the first test began. Vóra and Adonis asked me to be with them, watching the livestream. For the first time, people in town, besides us three, have seen the metal. It still looked rough, unpolished, unyielding, stubborn as it felt when I touched it and forged it for the first time. It has a loyalty, a personality, Doctor Anansi said that day. It felt wrong watching it, as if the metal did not want to be there, as if it didn't want to bend to human will. The screen was showing the laboratory, a few staff members watching and relaying to workstations, and in the centre, a pillar of blue tinted glass, illuminated from the inside, surrounded by a metal mesh, electrified. It took me a few moments to realise that there was no glass, and that was the metal's energy, cocooning the shard, trying to protect itself. As if it was alive.

The procedure started. Pre-written subtitles explained what the process consisted, and what where the steps they would take to open the shard of gravitonium. It did also mention that the particles of this specific gravitonium piece was originally encrypted and connected to the particles in a faraway spaceship, called the Precursor. If the experiment succeeded, they would be able to create a link between Earth and the craft in outer space.

After that, in the bottom right corner of the screen, a countdown appeared, and began to work its way down from sixty seconds. The staff members left the room, and the only thing remaining was the metal, a solitary blue glow. Forty-five seconds. The subtitle read "Initiate insertion", and a robotic arm entered the frame, holding what it looked like a scalpel. It passed through the exterior mesh and stopped just as it was about to touch the blue pillar of light and energy. Thirty seconds. "Insertion start", and the arm pushed through the blue barrier, which held it for a split second, but it let go. Twenty seconds. The arm stopped millimetres from touching the shard. Five seconds. Four, thee, two, one. "Insert". The metal arm pushed, touched the metal, which complaint, humming and spitting a gush of blue light. The automated arm kept pushing, and the metal kept holding. Until.

The screen died. Not just in the origin of the footage we realised, but everywhere. The pads stopped functioning, lights flickered and blew, and seconds later we felt the ground rumbling.

More out of instinct and reflex than anything else, I grabbed my knife. It had a sheath, a handle, a guard that I made myself, and it stood by me at all the time. I let my hand do what it needed to do, as I was unaware of the actual theory and comprehension of what was happening.

I stabbed the air, and counter to what I expected, I felt resistance. I saw the soft light coming out of the slim scar levitating in front of me. My hands pulled the knife down, still inside the floating wound, and it opened. A long, gleaming cut in the thin air. The three of us, mesmerised by what had just happened in the screen and now through the naked eye, didn't react. It was Vóra who jolting from her seat, said loudly.

"We have to go. Now!" She looked at her brother, who was still hypnotized by the beautiful light show. "Come Donis, quick" She managed to grab his arm, even having to support his weight as well as hers, with her healing leg. "Dia, open it up. Pull it open, quickly. We have to cross"

Cross? What, and to where? I looked at the two of them, moving towards me and the blue light scar. I looked down, to my knife, and twisted, and with the other hand, I fit it inside the wound, and pull it, spreading its borders.

Without thinking, I opened for Adonis and Vóra to jump inside, and I crossed right after. The rumbling got bigger, and the sounds were terrifyingly closer. My last thought before closing the wound, on the other side, was "Mal, I'm sorry".

***

EPILOGUE

The other side of the bright, glowing wound was devastation. We exited where we entered, but nothing was there anymore. In place of the apartment, of the whole building, the whole district, was rubble and debris. A dark, smoky sky, lit in shades of red and dark orange moved fast, with the wind blowing heavy dust and burnt leaves. We looked around, puzzled to what might had happened. I climbed down quickly, while Adonis helped Vóra. From where the two siblings lived, the river was hidden by a series of other buildings and houses, and further away, by the edge of the woods that bordered the town from the west and north, beyond the river itself. But then, there was nothing else blocking the view, to the dry empty river, to the flattened blocks of houses, and to the charcoal sticks bursting up from the ground where the pines once stood.

My eyes aimed at my own home, to Mal's, and at the rest of the buildings, it was destroyed, brought to the ground, only broken stone and visible steel skeletons. Following what was the river side, I moved my sight to my old house, the one the opposite side of the crater, the one with the crooked tree, but there was nothing. The workshop too, gone.

"Dia" Vóra called, and I turned to give her my hand as support for her to climb down the larger block of cement. "What is all this? Where are we?" She asked.

"I think" And I stopped, thinking, maybe waiting for a better answer, maybe waiting to confirm that that was true. "I think we are in the same place. We are at yours, but…"

And she pointed to the bottom of town, where the foundation was. This crater, immense, took over half of the lower district. No more foundation, no more old church, no more empty pool. The charred stone and wood still let loose sparks and embers, that would fly up and populate the dense, black cloud lingering above the hole. We walked down, slowly, afraid, and confused. The whole town looked dead and desolated. But we saw life still, lingering. Glimpses of people, far away, coming in and out of half broken buildings. Some stopped and looked, some ran away.

Vóra had her arms around me, and we walked slower, trying to find our footing through the mess of rock and stone. Adonis walked faster and reached the edge of the crater first. Much larger than the first, and much deeper too. A whole building could be hidden inside the gorge, without its highest floor peeking out. However, it hid a ship instead, and people gathered around it, scavenging and looting, some living inside of parts that were separated during the probable impact. Some of those people also seen us three, of those, some stared, some carried on. One looked and gazed, from the top of the structure, her eyes tired, her hair wild. I could not see the expression on her face, but I saw her chest moving, letting a far-away breath come out. She gave up and turned, crouched down and collected her parcels and bags, and walked away, to the other side of the ship. That was the last time we saw Anansi, as titles were meaningless.

The writings on the side of the ship were fading, but still quite visible. It read: *Precursor.*

ARIA

Book 1 of the Scintillance theory

Part of the Myth Herder Observatory Universe

ABOUT THE AUTHOR

Gyorgy lives in Bath, UK. He has worked for over fifteen years in academia and have a PhD in Anthropology. ARIA is his first published work outside of academia, and the beginning of this new chapter of his career. He also loves writing music and illustrating.

Twitter: @DrGyorgyNeto
Instagram: @writer.gyorgy
Website: gyorgyneto.wixsite.com/ghn-writer

Jostedalsbreen Publishing, 2021

Printed in Great Britain
by Amazon